TELLTALE SIGNS

TELLTALE SIGNS

A Savannah Williams Mystery

Debi Chestnut

Writers Club Press
New York Lincoln Shanghai

Telltale Signs

A Savannah Williams Mystery

Writers Club Press
an imprint of iUniverse, Inc.

For information address:
iUniverse, Inc.
2021 Pine Lake Road, Suite 100
Lincoln, NE 68512
www.iuniverse.com

ISBN: 0-595-25900-6 (pbk)
ISBN: 0-595-65418-5 (cloth)

Printed in the United States of America

To my husband, Lonnie, for his undying patience, my daughter Nichole, for her unwavering support, my friend and fellow writer, Beth Baldwin for never letting me quit, Tammy Lemmen, for her constant encouragement, and all my friends and fellow writers in Writer's Den.

*It's a pity you didn't know when you started
your game of murder, that I was playing it too.*
Robb White and William Castle,
House on Haunted Hill, (1958)

CHAPTER I

▼

The phone was ringing, unmercifully. I rolled over and looked at the clock. Two a.m. It was Saturday.

I grabbed the cordless. "This better be good."

"It's Jim. We have a situation."

Jim was the last person I wanted to talk to. He was a homicide detective that I had been living with. We had broken up two weeks ago and hadn't spoken since.

"What is it Jim?" I could hear the tenseness in his voice.

"A body was found about a half hour ago behind the shopping center at 23 and Gratiot. The victim's name is Robert Maxwell. He had one of your business cards in his pocket and a tarot card stabbed into his chest with a butterfly knife."

It really ticks me off when one of my clients gets killed. It's bad for business and makes it virtually impossible to bill.

I got out of bed amid the protestations of my dogs, Sydney, my Golden Retriever and Rambo, my Rottweiler, who had been comfortably curled up next to me.

I struggled to get my pink terry cloth robe on over my blue sweats and padded into the living room. Not exactly a fashion statement, but lately I had been sleeping alone. I flicked on a light and curled up in the corner of the couch.

"Why is it that every time there is a murder around here, you are involved in some way, shape, or form?" Jim asked in exasperation.

"Don't you use that tone of voice with me Jim Matthews." I responded curtly.

"Don't get testy. I was just kidding. Now, why don't you tell me why Mr. Maxwell consulted with you in the first place?"

"He thought his wife was cheating on him and he wanted me to prove it. I followed his wife one night last week and caught her going into a hotel with another man. Mr. Maxwell took it pretty hard."

I tried to keep my voice conversational, but the truth was I hadn't told Jim everything. I was wound up tighter than a drum. Mr. Maxwell had received a tarot card in the mail two days ago. There had been no return address on the envelope and Mr. Maxwell couldn't think of any reason why someone would send it to him.

"Did Mr. Maxwell know the man his wife was seeing? Which hotel?"

"He said he didn't recognize the man, and I am still working to identify him. They were at the Ashley Inn. What tarot card did the killer stab into Mr. Maxwell?"

"Why do you want to know? Your not keeping anything from me I should know about are you Savannah?" Jim's voice took on that macho cop tone. I hated that.

I had to think for a minute. Did he really need to know about the other tarot card? Probably. Did he need to know right now? No. Besides, I needed time to think.

"Just curious" I replied casually. "I recently took up tarot as a hobby." It wasn't exactly the truth, but it wasn't exactly a lie either.

"At the bottom of the card it says King of Swords. Mean anything to you?"

"Is the card right side up or upside down?" I asked reaching for a book lying on my marble topped coffee table.

"The card is right side up."

"The King of Swords is a judge. He has the power to command, the power of life and death. A king represents men. Does that help?" I asked.

"Yeah. I'm sure it helps a lot. I just don't know how yet. How do you do that anyway?"

"Do what?" I was used to Jim jumping from one subject to another. It was also a habit of mine. One I was trying to break.

"Rattle obscure information off the top of your head like that."

"I didn't. I have a book about the tarot on my coffee table. I looked it up. I got a book about the tarot in the mail yesterday. I don't know who sent it, but I think it might be Sandra. You know how she always sends me weird stuff. There was no return address on the envelope, but it was post marked Mt. Clements."

"I don't like this Savannah. There are too many coincidences. Listen, I know its real irregular, but since you're already involved as usual, why don't you come up to the scene. Maybe you can make some sense out of all this."

"Okay, I'll be there in about 15 minutes". I was wide-awake and all business now.

I ran into the bedroom, threw off my robe, grabbed the jeans and shirt that I had left crumpled on the floor.

Quickly getting dressed, I raced into the bathroom to wash my face and brush my teeth. I glanced at myself in the mirror. My face was pale, my eyes were puffy, and it was definitely going to be a bad hair day. Oh well, what do people expect in the middle of the night? In frustration I pulled my long auburn hair into a ponytail and headed out the door.

I hate it when my routine is altered. I usually sleep late on Saturdays. When I do manage to drag myself out of bed, I have my coffee and read the paper from cover to cover. Then I spend the rest of the day in my sweats watching TV. Not very productive, but necessary.

I was not a happy camper when I got to the scene. I slammed the door to my black jeep Cherokee and headed toward Jim who was standing just outside the yellow police tape that was strung around the perimeter of the crime scene. He was impeccably groomed and perfectly dressed in a pair of freshly pressed beige Dockers and navy blue polo shirt. His black, curly hair was neatly combed and his mustache perfectly trimmed. His bright, blue eyes were scanning the scene.

I went weak in the knees just looking at him. How does that man always manage to look so good no matter what time of day or night? I, on the other hand looked like something the cat wouldn't even drag in. My long curly hair would not cooperate and kept blowing in my face. My jeans and T-shirt were wrinkled and covered in assorted colors of dog hair.

"Savannah over here". Jim waved me over.

I walked up to Jim, and wordlessly he lifted the tape to allow me to pass onto the scene.

The crime scene itself was one of organized chaos. Evidence technicians were carefully photographing, tagging and bagging every piece of potential evidence they could find. Halogen lights had been set up and the scene was as bright as high noon on a sunny day. Someone handed me a cup of coffee as I passed under the tape.

"You look like you could use this." It was Ben Mills, Jim's partner. I must look worse than I thought.

Ben was well built with sandy blonde hair and his piercing brown eyes were framed with long thick eyelashes that women would kill for. He was also one of Ashley's most eligible bachelors.

"Thanks", I replied gratefully taking the coffee.

I scanned the scene trying to get a picture in my head. A light blue Dodge Shadow was parked about ten feet away from the crime scene and evidence techs were going over it with a fine toothcomb. I recognized the car as the one Mrs. Maxwell had driven to the hotel last week.

The dumpster itself was situated about 50 feet from the back of the building under a halogen light post. A thin layer of glass littered the area around the dumpster, and upon looking up, I noticed that the light had been broken. How convenient.

There was a pentagram spray painted in white about 10 feet in front of the dumpster with what appeared to be burnt candles placed at the points. Inside the pentagram there were some sort of symbols painted in red. Upon closer inspection, I realized the red paint was actually blood. Good thing I hadn't eaten yet. I then turned my attention to the dumpster itself.

My client was unceremoniously draped feet first over the dumpster. The lid was closed over his waist holding him in place. His long brown hair was hanging loose and his green eyes were open and staring into nothingness. He was wearing a white T-shirt that said, "Live long and prosper." There was irony somewhere, but it escaped me at the moment. The most prominent feature was the blue handled butterfly knife protruding from his chest holding the tarot card in place.

The Medical Examiner had arrived and was waiting for the okay to remove the body. It was Cal Bowers. Good man. He was thorough and careful.

Cal greeted me with a smile. "Hey Savannah. How's it going?"

"Just fine Cal. Good to see you. Let's see what we've got?"

Cal and one of his technicians laid a black body bag on a gurney in front of the dumpster. Carefully they removed the body from the dumpster and laid it on the bag. I could now see that he was wearing a pair of worn blue jeans and black cowboy boots. He had on a black belt with a Harley Davidson belt buckle. Cal then began a cursory examination of the body. I decided it was time to have a closer look the dumpster. Besides, dead bodies make me squeamish.

After borrowing a flashlight from one of the officers on the scene, I took a quick glance inside the dumpster.

The light landed on something red, white and furry. After stifling a scream and controlling the wave of nausea that washed through my body, I steeled myself and took another look.

Inside the dumpster lay the body of a white cat with its throat cut. It didn't take a giant leap of faith to figure out where the blood came from.

"Savannah? Jim? Can you two come over here please?" It was Cal. Maybe he found out something interesting about our Mr. Maxwell. I notified one of the crime scene personnel about the cat and walked over to the gurney.

"Here's what we've got so far." Cal began, "Mr. Maxwell was shot at point blank range execution style in the back of the head. Judging from the entrance wound I would guess he was shot with a small caliber semi-automatic pistol, but I won't know for sure until after the autopsy. The tarot card and knife were inserted shortly after death. There are no signs of a struggle, or defensive wounds that I can see right now. Judging by his body temperature and the weather today, I would say he has been dead approximately three to five hours. If there's nothing else you two need, I am going to take Mr. Maxwell back to the morgue and get started. I should have a preliminary report to you in about four to six hours."

Jim and I glanced at each other. "There's nothing else I need Cal. Thanks. Jim, what about you?"

"No, I'm finished here."

"Listen, Jim, I know it's highly irregular and probably breaking a lot of rules and I have no business asking, but could I get a copy of the crime scene video? Those symbols in the pentagram seem familiar somehow, and I would like to be able to study them. Besides, he was my client and I feel kind of responsible."

"Look Savannah, you know I can't do that, but I've got an idea." Jim strode over to one of the crime scene photographers. I saw the photographer load a fresh roll of film into a camera and hand it to Jim, who walked over to the pentagram and snapped five or six pictures from different angles. After rewinding the film, Jim popped it out and handed the camera back to the technician. He returned to where I was standing.

"Remember, you call me first if you find something, and I want a copy of the photo of the man who met Mrs. Maxwell. Got it?" He said sternly as he placed the roll of film into my hand.

"Got it. Thanks Jim. I'll drop a copy of the picture by the station. Has anybody notified the next of kin?" I asked stifling a yawn.

"I'm on the way over there now. I swear Savannah this is the worst part of the job." For the first time all morning Jim looked tired. Murder does that to you.

"I know. Listen, I'm going to go home and grab a couple of hours sleep. I'll talk to you at later."

To tell the truth, I couldn't wait to climb back into bed, I was whipped. My eyelids felt like lead and a headache was beginning to manifest itself behind my left eye. I turned to head back to my jeep. Jim grabbed my arm and I felt his touch rush through me like a shot of adrenaline. It pissed me off that he still could still have that effect on my body.

"Savannah, listen. I've been doing a lot of thinking these past two weeks. I really think we need to talk. Can we grab a cup of coffee?"

I shook my arm free of his grasp. "Jim. Look. As much as I would like to hear what you have to say, it is 6:30 in the morning. I have been up half the night, I'm exhausted, and may I point out, in case you have forgotten, that you are in the middle of a murder investigation. Not to mention the press is beginning to descend on us like a swarm of locusts. You're timing, as usual, is a little off. Now, if you don't need me for anything else, I am going home. Goodnight."

With that, I turned on my heel and walked away. Not daring to look back, and not wanting him to see the tears that were welling up in my eyes. I sidestepped the press, climbed into my jeep and headed out of the parking lot, fast.

While I am heading back home, I should probably introduce myself. My name is Savannah Williams. I am thirty-three years old and single. I stand about five feet nothing and have long, curly auburn hair, which, if you talk to people who know me, will report that it matches my temper. They are probably right. I entered the FBI right out of college and became a profiler. I was partnered with a wonderful man named Frank Roth. We were partners, friends and lovers. Unfortunately a serial killer who has yet to be apprehended murdered him in cold blood seconds after I had dropped him off at home. Not being able to forgive myself and wracked with grief, I suffered what the doctors termed an emotional breakdown. After three months of recovery and several hospitalizations, I walked into FBI headquarters, packed up my office, turned in my badge and walked away. I then moved here and became a private investigator. That was two years ago. I still have some shaky moments, but am doing okay.

CHAPTER 2

▼

I pulled into my driveway, only to find my friend Sandra's BMW parked there. I had given her a key in case of an emergency, but to Sandra a broken fingernail could constitute an emergency. With a heavy sigh, I opened the front door and walked in.

Sandra was sitting at my kitchen table impeccably dressed in a black Christian Dior pantsuit eating an apple turnover, sipping freshly brewed coffee, and reading my morning paper. Sydney and Rambo were sprawled on my new Hunter green sofa, happily devouring a donut.

"Savannah, where have you been? You look like hell. What are you doing up so early?" The words were barely intelligible through her bites of turnover.

"Shopping. Gee thanks, and I was called to an apparent murder scene at four o'clock this morning. What are you doing here? Why are Sydney and Rambo on my new couch, and why are they eating donuts?"

"I came to visit, they wanted to be and they wanted one. Now," Sandra leaned forward conspiratorially, "grab a cup of coffee and a turnover, sit down and tell me about the murder." Her emerald green eyes were sparkling with excitement. If there's one thing Sandra liked, it was a good murder.

"Sandra, I really don't want to talk about it right now. I don't mean to be rude, but I need to take a nap, grab a shower, and try to find out why one of my clients was killed."

"The victim was one of your clients? I swear Savannah, every time there's a murder around here it seems like you are in the middle of it. Why bother sleeping now? It's almost 7:00. Go take a shower while I watch the news. It will make you feel better. After your shower I can tell you all the gossip you are missing by living out in the country." Sandra reached for the remote control with one hand and another turnover with the other.

Resigned to the fact that Sandra was going to stay put, and I was going to suffer through a day of sleep deprivation, I sighed and headed for the shower. At least I would have a few minutes to gather my thoughts and sift through the multitudes of possible clues left at the scene.

In fact, I thought as I stepped into the shower, allowing the soothing hot water to run over me, there were almost too many clues, too much left behind by the killer. He was either sloppy or taunting us. I immediately ruled out sloppy. No, this killer was very organized, very careful. There was nothing at the scene he didn't want found. My mind kept going back to the symbols written in blood. I recognized them from somewhere, I just couldn't remember where. What about the tarot card? Did it represent the killer or the victim?

Stalling for about as long as I could, I turned off the shower and grabbed a hot towel from the towel warmer. I then sauntered into the bedroom to get dressed. Sydney and Rambo had removed themselves from my sofa and were now lying on my bed munching on another donut.

I strode out into the kitchen. "Sandra, why did you give Sydney and Rambo another donut? You know I'm trying to wean them from people food."

"Savannah dear," Sandra gave me a pitying look and shook her head sadly, "Sydney and Rambo are two years old. It's a little too late for that. You know you can't teach an old dog new tricks, which is exactly why your and Jim's relationship didn't work out. You wanted him to change too much."

"Excuse me. I wanted him to change? What about him wanting me to start jogging with him? What about him wanting me to become a vegetarian? What about him wanting me to wear something different besides jeans and sweatshirts? What about him wanting me to quit smoking?" I said as I reached for a cigarette and lit it in defiance. "I'm sorry, but it sounds to me like I was the one who was expected to do all the changing."

I was getting really wound up and began pacing the kitchen. "And get this, as I was leaving the crime scene he had the nerve to say that he had been thinking, that we needed to talk, and could we go have a cup of coffee? Do you believe that? He walks out on me without any good reason and thinks that just because he gives me that irresistible puppy dog look with those sexy, blue eyes that I will ask how high when he says jump. I think not". I finished with a flourish as I grabbed my freshly poured cup of coffee and sat down at the table.

Sandra had silently watched me storm around the kitchen ranting and raving. Carefully, she placed her coffee cup on the table, took a moment to examine her perfectly manicured nails, gave me her best shame on you look and finally, after what seemed like an eternity, spoke.

"My, my, aren't we the self-righteous little thing today? He really wanted to go for coffee and talk? Why on earth didn't you go? What's wrong with you?"

"Sandra, we were at a crime scene, a murder had just been committed, the next of kin needed to be notified, the press was circling us like sharks in a feeding frenzy, and you ask why I wouldn't take the time to go have coffee?"

"So, basically what you're saying is that you were afraid that he would tell you that he just wanted to be friends, and he was sorry if he hurt you. Right?" Sandra had a way of cutting through the bull and hitting the bullseye every time.

"Yes. Now, catch me up on the gossip." I felt it was best to change the subject. Sandra was hitting too close to home.

I walked Sandra to the door at about 10:00. She was still chatting away when I opened the door for her.

"Oh, by the way. Rita found a great new psychic. She swears by her. I'm going to see her myself. Why don't you come with? It will be great fun. Rita says that she reads palms, crystals, and tea leaves, but her specialty is tarot cards."

"Tarot cards? Where are the readings held?" Buzzers and whistles were going off madly in my head. "And speaking of tarot cards, why did you send me that book?"

"What book? What are you talking about?" I could tell by the baffled look on Sandra's face that she had no clue what I was talking about.

"I got a book about tarot cards in the mail a couple of days ago. I just assumed you had sent it to me." Now I was confused.

If Sandra hadn't sent the book, it only meant one thing. The killer had. But why?

"I'm sorry Sandra. Someone else must have sent it. Now what were you saying about Rita's new psychic?"

"Madame Phoebe has a shop not too far from here. Mt. Clements I think Rita said. Why she couldn't find a good psychic closer to home is beyond me, but you know Rita. Anyway, Rita said that she has an occult bookstore and does the readings in the back. Interested?"

"Maybe. I'll give you a call." Without trying to be rude, I practically pushed Sandra out the door, grabbed my car keys and purse and headed out the door. I had to check this place out for myself.

Downtown Mt. Clements is a quaint place filled with small town charm. It is a close-knit community of friendly, hard working people. Wonderful small stores and restaurants adorn the tree-lined streets.

It took a little time, but I finally found Madame Phoebe's New Age Bookstore.

I entered the store and was immediately overwhelmed by the smell of sandalwood incense. A small woman with black hair, and large hoop earrings stood behind the counter. I judged her to be in her early to late 30's. She looked very pleasant and serene, but I noticed that her eyes never stopped moving as she scanned the customers.

The store was neatly arranged with bookshelves lining the walls. Display cabinets were placed neatly in the middle of the store. Two dark green and burgundy overstuffed chintz chairs were situated in the back corner of the store inviting people to sit and browse through the vast selection of titles and subjects offered. A black cat was curled up comfortably in one of the chairs, and he opened his gorgeous, gold eyes to determine if I was worth bothering with. Evidently I wasn't, because after a long, luxurious yawn, he settled back down to his nap.

The store emitted an aura of mystery and enticed patrons to explore the unknown. After browsing through the crystals, incense, tools for Wicca worship, Satan worship, and every other obscure religion, quite frankly, I had the creeps. Nonetheless, the store somehow drew you in and cast a spell that forced you to go deeper and explore every nook and cranny.

I headed for a large shelf of books at the back of the store, and soon became totally engrossed in a book about poltergeists and ghosts. I had sunk into one of the chintz chairs and the black cat had somehow planted himself on my lap and was emitting an awesome purr as my hand absently stroked his soft, silky coat. I was so caught up in my book, that I didn't even hear the sales clerk approach my chair.

"Can I help you find something?" Her voice was soft and sweet. After peeling myself off the ceiling, and sending the cat flying, I stood and addressed this funny little woman.

"Yes, I am interested in a book about tarot cards. Do you carry any?"

"Well of course. Do you read the tarot?" She was trying desperately to hide the smile playing around her mouth after having scared me half to death and the cat out of three of its nine lives.

"Not until recently." It wasn't quite a lie, but it was close. "Are you Madame Phoebe?"

"Why yes." She seemed pleased that I had heard of her. "Why do you ask?"

"A friend of mine came here for a reading. She spoke very highly of you" A little flattery never hurt.

"How nice. I'm glad she was pleased. Now, about your book. They are right over here."

Madame Phoebe led me to a shelf of books along the opposite wall. I immediately noticed that there were several books just like the one I had received in the mail.

"What about this one?" I reached for the book and began to skim through it.

"It's a very good book. I just got them in last week and have already sold two of them."

"Really, do you mind if I ask who bought them?" I tried to keep my voice conversational. "I know several people who are interested in the tarot."

"Well, let me think a minute." Her small face crinkled up in thought. "There was a woman, about your age, and a man came in and bought the other one a couple of days ago. He was in his mid to late thirties. Do they sound like someone you would know?"

"Um, no, not that I can think of." After looking through a few more tarot card books I finally chose one different than the one I had received in the mail. A different prospective couldn't' hurt. As I paid for the book I glanced at my watch. "Oh my God, I didn't realize it was so late. I have an urgent appointment I must get to. Thanks for your help."

As I turned to go, Madame Phoebe reached out and took my hand. She turned it over and looked at my palm. Her face suddenly became very serious and she leaned close to me.

"My dear, you are in great danger from one close to you. Be careful whom you trust. I am very worried about you"

I eased my hand out of hers. "Thanks for your concern, but I really must go."

I breezed gracefully out the door and raced for my jeep. I slid behind the wheel, still reeling over Madame Phoebe's words. What if I really was the target? No, that was ridiculous. If I was the target, I would be the one who would be dead. Wouldn't I?

I left Madame Phoebe's and was almost home when I remembered I had a meeting with a new client at the Log Cabin Restaurant close to town.

I walked into the restaurant, requested a table in the smoking section and ordered a cup of coffee. A few minutes later a tall, well-built handsome man of about forty approached my table.

"Ms. Williams?" He asked tentatively.

I nodded my head in assent.

"I'm Roger Walker"

"Mr. Walker. Please sit down and call me Savannah."

"Thank you." He responded as he slid into the booth across from me.

The waitress approached with my coffee and Mr. Walker ordered one for himself. Once it had been delivered and we ordered lunch, I withdrew a pad of paper and pen from my briefcase.

"What can I do for you Mr. Walker?" I asked, with my pen poised over the paper.

"Please call me Roger." He replied, nervously taking a sip of his coffee. "I think my wife is having an affair and I want you to find out."

"No problem. What makes you think your wife is cheating on you?" I asked sipping my coffee.

"I travel a lot for my job, and sometimes when I call home at night she isn't there, or if she is, she doesn't answer the phone. When I ask her about it, she always has a plausible excuse, but I just need to be sure. Understand?"

Our food arrived and I carefully jellied a piece of toast as I responded.

"I understand. Do you have a recent picture of your wife?"

Mr. Walker reached into his shirt pocket and handed me a photograph. I showed a small, pretty woman about my age with long blonde hair and pretty blue eyes. I put the picture in my briefcase.

We spent the next forty-five minutes or so eating and talking. I ascertained Mrs. Walker's usual schedule. Mr. Walker also told me he wouldn't be going out of town for another few weeks and promised to call me the night before he left. He had no problem with my rates, so after we ate I picked up the tab and headed home.

CHAPTER 3

▼

By the time I got home it was noon. I picked up the mail that had been dropped through the mail slot by the front door and tossed it on the kitchen counter. Sydney and Rambo were doing a little dance by the back door, so I opened it and followed them outside onto the deck. The late summer afternoon was warm and sunny. A soft breeze was blowing and carried the fresh scent of lilacs.

When the dogs were ready to come back in, I fed them and headed to my bedroom. I knew I needed to get to work on those symbols, but I needed sleep more. I kicked off my tennis shoes and flopped down on the bed.

It was six o'clock when I woke up. I took a shower, put on my robe and made my way into the kitchen to find something to eat. I popped a frozen dinner into the microwave and sat down at the kitchen table to go through my mail. I came upon a plain, white envelope with the word "Savannah" typed on the front. There was no return address and no postmark. A mixture of fear and adrenaline surged through my body as I held the envelope. Hesitantly, I opened it and withdrew a sheet of white paper. On it was a neatly typed message:

Savannah,

I thought I would drop this off personally. The postal service just seems so impersonal. I hope the book I sent you was helpful. It's one of my favorites. Keep it close. Chances are you will need it again.

It was unsigned. A cold chill ran down my body as I read the contents. I immediately raced through the house double checking the doors and windows and closing all the blinds. I grabbed the phone and tried to steady my hand long enough to call Jim. I was midway through dialing when I slammed the phone back onto the receiver. I was not going to run to him just because I was scared. That would give him the impression that I still needed him. I would take the note to him tomorrow.

As I slammed the phone down, I noticed the light was blinking on my answering machine. I pushed the button and braced myself, expecting to hear the voice of the killer.

"Ms. Williams, this is Mrs. Maxwell, could you please telephone me as soon as possible? My number is 555-3481. Thank you."

What on earth is up with that I wondered and without hesitation dialed Mrs. Maxwell's number and made an appointment to meet with her later tonight.

I walked back into the kitchen, poured a glass of wine, and grabbed the crime scene photos I had developed on my way back from Madame Phoebe's. With newfound determination, I headed into the den to piece together what I knew about Mr. Maxwell's murder.

My den is two stories tall. The first floor consists of a very large, antique library table that I use as a desk, as well as several file cabinets that are stuffed with files of old cases and other information from when I worked at the FBI as a profiler. My computer sits on a small, antique mahogany table alongside my desk. Luxurious hunter green and gold oriental rugs grace the hardwood floors. The second story of the den is lined with bookshelves. A spiral staircase was installed that winds up to a catwalk so that I have access to the bookshelves. After retrieving Mr. Maxwell's file, I sat down in my cozy burgundy leather office chair and got down to work.

The first item I pulled out was the tarot card Mr. Maxwell had received in the mail two days ago. The card had been glued upside down to a stiff piece of cardboard. The card itself was the Page of Swords and according to the tarot book this meant that there was a tendency to frivolity and cunning. An imposter was likely to be exposed. There was also a possibility of ill health and to be prepared for the unexpected.

I surmised that the Page of Swords had been a warning to Mr. Maxwell, but about what? Who was the imposter? Mr. Maxwell or the murderer? The King of Swords must represent the killer who sees himself as having the power of life and death.

I pulled out the photo I had taken of the man who was with Mrs. Maxwell at the hotel and slipped it and the tarot card Mr. Maxwell had received, into a separate file folder. I sat back in my chair, lit a cigarette and slowly sipped my wine. Oh yeah, Mrs. Maxwell and I had a lot to talk about this evening.

I arrived early for my appointment with Mrs. Maxwell. I parked my jeep in St. Anthony's Church parking lot and had a clear view of the house, which was a well-kept older ranch close to downtown Ashley. Just as I parked my car, I observed the man in the photograph with Mrs. Maxwell come out of the house and carefully look around. I took a dive in my front seat and cautiously peered up over the dashboard. Satisfied that everything was as it should be, the man got into an older blue Ford pick-up and quickly drove away. It was too dark to make out the license plate of the truck as it sped out of sight.

Straightening myself out, I exited the jeep and made my way up to the house. A small, petite woman of about 24 answered the door. She had mousy brown hair, big brown eyes, and was dressed in blue jeans and a gray sweatshirt.

I introduced myself and was led into a sparsely furnished living room. A plaid couch of multi-colored browns and tan, a cheap imitation leather recliner, two garage sale end tables, and a TV on an old chest of drawers made up the furnishings. Mrs. Maxwell sunk onto the sofa, so I took the recliner. Neither one of us had spoken, we had spent the last three or four minutes sizing each other up. I decided to be the first one to break the silence.

"Mrs. Maxwell, why did you contact me?" I asked gently. She seemed fragile somehow.

"The detective who told me about Robbie said that your card was found in Robbie's pocket. I wanted to know why?" A somewhat defiant look flashed across her face that she quickly checked. Maybe Mrs. Maxwell wasn't as fragile as she looked.

I took a moment before answering. I wasn't sure what cards I wanted to play and how. I formed my words carefully as I answered and withdrew the tarot card Mr. Maxwell had received out of the file folder, "Robbie had received this tarot card in the mail a few days ago. He wanted me to find out who sent it." It wasn't the whole truth, but it was truthful. I held the card out toward her and she took it from my hand and studied it for a few minutes before handing it back and turning her attention to me.

"Did you find out? Who sent it I mean."

"No, I haven't found out exactly who sent it, but I have a few ideas. Have you seen this card before?" I wanted to keep the ball in her court.

"Yes. Robbie showed it to me when it arrived. We couldn't figure out who sent it or why." She looked deep into my eyes, begging for answers I couldn't give her.

"Mrs. Maxwell, tell me about Robbie. Who were his friends, his enemies, what did he like to do?"

"Robbie was a kind, decent man. We've only been married for two years. We met in high school. He doesn't, um, I mean he didn't have many friends and I can't imagine him having any enemies. Robbie loved to hunt and fish, but he worked so much he didn't have much time for it, or me." A touch of bitterness had crept into her voice.

I decided it was time to change the subject. "Mrs. Maxwell, tell me where Robbie was going the night he was killed."

"We had a fight and Robbie stormed out of the house. I don't know where he was heading, but if I had to guess I would say he headed up to the Stop Light Tavern to have a few beers. A few of his friends usually hang out there."

"What did you and Robbie fight about?"

"We fought about the usual things. You know, how he's never here, money, you name it. We fought about it. I feel so bad you know? I mean the last words Robbie and I said to each other were in anger." I could hear the regret in her voice.

I carefully replaced the card in the file folder and pulled out the photograph of her and the mystery man I had taken at the hotel.

"Mrs. Maxwell, is the man in this picture what you and Robbie fought about that night?" I watched her response carefully.

She took the photograph and I saw the fear well up in her eyes. She brought herself under control remarkably fast. Impressive.

"Where did you get this?" There was a slight tone of indignation in her voice.

"I took it last week. Who is this man Mrs. Maxwell?" I decided to press a little bit.

Mrs. Maxwell practically leapt off the couch and started to pace the small room. Without warning she turned to face me, her eyes full of anger, her voice loud and harsh.

"This man has nothing to do with Robbie's death. He is just a friend of mine. This is the real reason Robbie hired you isn't it? He hired you to follow me didn't he?"

"Mrs. Maxwell," I said, keeping my voice calm, "I never implied that the man in the photograph killed Robbie. I simply asked who he was."

"He has nothing to do with any of this. He is just a friend." The indignation had crept back into her voice as she handed the photograph back to me.

I slipped the photograph into the file folder. "Mrs. Maxwell, I know that you met this man at a hotel. I know that Robbie confronted you about it, and I also know that you two had a huge argument. Now Robbie's been murdered and you won't identify the man you were with. Doesn't that sound just a little bit suspicious to you?"

"I know how it looks, but that is not the reason Robbie was murdered."

Mrs. Maxwell had regained her composure and had taken up her position on the couch.

"Then what is the reason, Mrs. Maxwell? Tell me, why do you think Robbie was killed?"

"I don't know. I just don't know." Tears had welled up in her eyes. "I don't care what you think of me, but in my own way, I really loved Robbie and I'm sorry he's dead. He deserved better."

Looking her right in the eye I responded, "Yes he did Mrs. Maxwell."

I rose to leave.

"Thank you for your time Mrs. Maxwell. I can let myself out."

Satisfied that I had rattled her cage enough for one day, I left the house and walked back to my jeep. Knowing that she was probably watching me from the window, I started my jeep and drove out of the parking lot. I drove around the block and parked down the street. I cut the engine and sat back to wait.

I didn't have to wait long. Within fifteen minutes the blue pick-up reappeared and I watched it pull into Mrs. Maxwell's driveway. The man got out and I saw Mrs. Maxwell in the doorway waiting to let him in.

I fished my cell phone out of my purse and dialed Jim's number. He answered on the second ring.

"Jim Matthews." His voice sounded tired.

"Jim. It's Savannah. I'm parked outside the Maxwell house. The man in the photograph just went inside".

"I'm on the way. Now get out of there. Damn it Savannah, what were you doing there in the first place?" I could hear the exasperation in his voice.

"I was in the neighborhood." I replied flatly and disconnected before Jim could ask me any more questions. I had some answers, but not the ones I was looking for.

The meeting with Mrs. Maxwell had been unsettling and I wasn't any closer to discovering who the mystery man was. Maybe Jim would have better luck.

Mrs. Maxwell had said that Robbie usually hung out at the Stop Light Tavern. So I decided to check it out on my way home.

I wandered in, found a seat at the bar and ordered a beer. There was a man standing next to me who appeared as if he could have been the model for a Ford van. He was wearing a faded pair of jeans, cowboy boots and a T-Shirt. He was talking to a smaller man, dressed in a similar fashion. The topic of the night seemed to be Robbie's murder.

"I'm sorry," I said demurely, "I couldn't help but overhear you talking about Robbie Maxwell's murder. Did you guys know him?"

Both men looked at me cautiously. "Yeah, we knew him. Why do you want to know?"

I decided the best thing to do was play it straight.

"I'm a private detective. My name is Savannah Williams. Robbie consulted me on another matter about 2 weeks before he was killed. I feel kind of responsible, he being my client and all, and I am trying to find out who killed him and why."

They digested this information for a few minutes and finally, deciding that I was telling the truth, the big man spoke.

"Name's Bobby Kramer," motioning to the other man with him he said, "This here's my brother Russ. Robbie and I grew up together. He was a good guy. What do you want to know?"

"Were you two up here the night Robbie was killed?"

"Yeah we were up here. Robbie came in about 10:00. He and his wife had a fight and Robbie was pretty upset."

"Did Robbie say what they fought about?"

"Yeah, seems Robbie found out that Tabby was having an affair with someone. Robbie didn't know who he was and it was making him crazy." Bobby shook his head in disgust. "How she could do that to him is beyond me. He was nuts about her."

"Tabby? You mean Mrs. Maxwell?"

"Yeah, her real name is Tabitha, but everyone calls her Tabby."

"Did Robbie talk to anyone else while he was here?"

"Not that we saw. We left about 11:00 and Robbie was still here. Sorry we can't be more help. Maybe Barb knows something. She was bartending that night. Hey Barb, come here for a minute." Bobby motioned to the bartender.

Barb came over to where we were. She was a small woman with short blonde hair. I judged her to be somewhere in her early to late thirties to early forties. Not pretty, but cute.

"Do you guys need another one?" Her voice was soft and sweet. I liked her immediately.

"Listen Barb. This here's Savannah." Bobby motioned to me and I nodded a greeting. "She's a private detective. She's trying to find out who killed Robbie. Did you see Robbie talking to anyone after we left the other night?"

Barb took a minute to think. I was waiting with bated breath. I was getting close to something here. I could feel it.

"Well, let's see. You guys left and Robbie ordered another beer. I talked to him for a few minutes and then this guy I didn't recognize, who was sitting down the bar, started to talk to him. I got busy after that and don't remember anything else."

"This guy Robbie was talking to. Do you remember what he looked like?" I could hardly contain my excitement.

"No, not really. He wasn't bad looking I remember that. Oh and he was drinking rum and coke. I think he had dark hair, but as I said, I was pretty busy that night and didn't pay much attention. Sorry."

"That's okay. Do you remember what time Robbie or this other man left?"

"Robbie left around midnight and I think the other guy left around the same time, but I couldn't be sure."

"Did you hear what Robbie and this man were talking about?"

"I caught bits and pieces. Mostly they were singing the woman done me wrong song. I think they were just commiserating with each other. Robbie was pretty upset when he came in here and was talking pretty loud for awhile."

"Do you remember anything else?"

"You know, now that you mention it. Robbie had been in a few nights before that and said that he had hired a private detective to follow Tabby and that the detective had taken a picture of Tabby and another man coming out of a hotel. That was you wasn't it?"

"Guilty as charged". I replied, laughing. "Listen, I have a picture in the car I need you guys to look at. Would you do that for me?"

All of them nodded yes and I ran out to my jeep to retrieve the picture of Tabby and the mystery man. I reentered the bar and showed the picture to Russ, Bobby and Barb.

"Do any of you recognize the man in this picture?"

All three of them studied the picture carefully.

Bobby spoke up first. "I've seen him around town, but I don't know who he is. Do you think he killed Robbie?"

I was entering dangerous territory here. The last thing I wanted was for a vigilante group to hunt this man down. I formed my answer carefully.

"There is no evidence that points to this man as being the killer. I just want to talk to him. Quite frankly, I don't think he is, but I need to make sure. Barb? Do you know him?"

"No, at least I don't think so. I see so many people it's hard to remember all of them. I'll watch for him now though."

"Listen guys, it's getting late. Here is my card. If any of you think of anything else please call me." I handed one of my cards to each of them, paid my tab and got up to go.

"Savannah," Bobby spoke up "if you need any help just call Barb here, she knows where to find me. Okay?"

"You got it, and thanks." I left the bar and headed for home.

As I rounded the corner, I saw Jim's black Durango in my driveway. For a brief second I thought about hiding out until he left, but I knew Jim was persistent and wouldn't leave until he talked to me. Funny, I saw more of him now then when we were dating.

Jim was sitting on the bench by my front door and rose when I approached.

"Where in the hell have you been? I've been worried sick."

Deciding to dodge the question, I answered it with a question. "Did you talk to the mystery man?" I unlocked the front door. I wasn't in the mood for company, least of all his.

"There was no answer at the door and the truck was gone when I got there." Jim followed me in the house, walked into the kitchen and got a beer out of the refrigerator. Wordlessly, he held up a bottle of wine. I nodded and he poured me a glass. He handed me my glass, headed into the great room and made himself comfortable on the couch. I had no choice but to follow. It was going to be a long night. I followed him into the great room and settled in one of the recliners. I took a sip of wine, grabbed my cigarettes off the table next to the chair and lit one.

"Must you." There was a note of disgust in his voice.

"Yes I must." I was getting testy. I was tired and just wanted to go to bed. "Other than wanting to tell me you missed the mystery man, which you could have done over the phone, is there any reason for your visit?"

"The Chief wanted me to talk to you about consulting as a profiler on the case. You were, are, the best in the business and we could really use your help."

"I don't do that anymore. You know that. When I quit the FBI after Frank was murdered, that was it. Done. Finished. That part of my life is over. No discussion." I purposely kept my voice firm.

"I told the Chief that Savannah, I really did. But honestly, don't you think you should let go of the past? I know Frank was your partner and that you were really tight. And I can only imagine how devastated you were when he was murdered, but it's been 2 years Savannah, don't you think it's time you got back on the horse?"

"No Jim. I don't think you can imagine what it was like for me when Frank was murdered. Don't you get it? Frank's murderer was the only serial killer case I worked on where I couldn't get a clear profile. I was helpless, and the fact that he has never been caught will haunt me until the day I die." I was fighting hard to keep control. I could feel the tears welling up in my eyes.

Jim got off the couch and came over to where I was sitting. He took my hands and slowly pulled me out of the chair enveloping me in a bear hug.

"I'm so sorry Savannah. I should have followed my better judgment and never brought it up, but I promised the Chief I would ask."

I barely heard him. I was fighting for control, but at the same time breathing in the scent of him, woodsy and masculine. I felt safe and warm wrapped up in his arms. I raised my head off his shoulder and looked into his eyes. He buried his hand in my long thick, auburn hair and staring deeply into my eyes, kissed me, gently at first, and then the kisses became greedier. My head was spinning and my body felt like it was on fire. Finally, my brain overruled my hormones and I pulled away from him wiping my mouth on the sleeve of my sweater.

We stood staring at each other panting and breathless. Finally he spoke, "I am so sorry Savannah. I didn't mean for that to happen. It's just…"

"I know, but I think you should leave now. It has been a long day and I'm tired. Tell the Chief I'll think about it." I led him to the door and opened it for him.

"I'm sorry Savannah." Jim gave me one last pleading look before he walked out the door. I watched him get into his truck and drive away.

"You could have stayed if you had asked." I said quietly as I shut and locked the door.

I walked into the kitchen, poured another glass of wine and thought about Frank. We had been partners, friends and lovers for six years while we were in the FBI. We had been working on a case that involved a serial killer that was haunting the streets of Baltimore, and could not get a clear profile of him.

The night Frank was killed; I had dropped him off at about four in the morning to get some sleep. As I drove away, I heard a shot ring out. By the time I stopped the car and ran back to Frank's, it was too late. He was lying dead in the doorway. The serial killer disappeared that day. Two weeks later, after suffering what the doctors termed as a "nervous breakdown", I turned in my badge, packed up my office and walked away.

I wandered into the den to make some notes about my visit with Mrs. Maxwell and my conversations at the bar. As I was cleaning up my desk, I came back across the note I had received in the mail from the killer. Damn, I had forgotten to tell Jim about it. Oh well, there were a lot of things I had forgotten to mention to Jim.

CHAPTER 4

▼

I usually love Sundays, but this one was shaping up to be a bad one. I got up early, let the dogs out and made a pot of coffee. I sat down at the kitchen table with my coffee and *Macomb Times*, the local paper. I opened it only to find Mr. Maxwell's murder splashed all over the front-page, along with a picture of Jim and me talking at the crime scene. So much for anonymity. I couldn't blame the reporter, he was only doing his job, but I would have preferred he'd used another picture. Tossing the paper aside, I poured another cup of coffee and made my way into the bedroom to take a shower and figure out what course of action to take next.

I got dressed, and as I do every Sunday morning, headed out the door to take the dogs for a romp in the woods.

We walked out of the subdivision and up Sass Road about a half-mile. We crossed 24 Mile Road and entered the thick woods. I let the dogs off their leashes and they scampered off happily to chase squirrels and explore.

I sat down on a tree stump to think. I don't know how long I sat there, but suddenly I heard a rifle shot. I felt something whiz by my head and lodge itself in the tree next to me. I screamed, hit the floor of the woods, and started to crawl through the thick underbrush toward a big tree, dodging two or three more shots as I made my way to cover.

Cautiously, I peered out from behind the tree and caught a glimpse of someone dressed in fatigues, carrying a hunting rifle and running out of the woods about 100 feet away.

The dogs, hearing my scream, came crashing through the woods and started licking my face as I sat down against the tree to catch my breath. From somewhere in the distance I heard the sound of a car start up and take off down the road.

Knowing that I was probably safe, I got up and examined the tree where the first bullet had impacted itself. I dug my penknife out of my pocket and carefully extracted what was left of the bullet. I then walked over to where the shooter had been standing and found three shell casings lying on the ground. After gathering the casings, I put the dogs back on their leashes and gingerly made my way out of the woods. I had gotten someones attention, but whose?

As I was walking back to the house I started to shake. The reality of almost being killed was starting to sink in. When I was almost home, I saw Jim's Durango pull in my driveway. How does he always know when I need him? He saw me with the dogs and got out of the car and headed down the sidewalk toward me. Without hesitation, I ran down the sidewalk and threw myself into his arms sobbing.

"Whoa, whoa hey what's going on? What's wrong? Are you okay?" His arms were wrapped tightly around me as he walked me up to the house. He took my keys, unlocked the front door and led me into the house. He gave the dogs some water and got me a tissue. By this time I had pretty much regained my composure and was thoroughly ticked off at myself for falling apart like that. I had been shot at before and never reacted like that.

Jim kneeled on the floor in front of my chair. "Okay, now what happened? Start at the beginning."

"I took the dogs for their usual run through the woods and someone shot at me with a rifle." I began, choking back sobs as I spoke. "I couldn't get a good look at who it was. All I know is that he was wearing fatigues. What are you doing here?"

"Someone called 911 and said that you had been shot at. I heard the call go out on the police radio so I headed over here. The call originated from a pay phone at the drug store up the street. Damn it Savannah, what is going on here?" Jim ran his hands through his curly, dark hair in frustration.

I decided it was time I came clean with Jim. I told him about the other tarot card that Mr. Maxwell had received and about my visit with Mrs. Maxwell from the night before. I didn't tell him about my visit to the Stop Light Tavern, about the note I got in the mail, or that the shell casings and bullet were safely tucked away in my pocket. A girl's got to have some secrets.

Jim was pretty mad at me for withholding information, but as we talked, he calmed down.

"Look Jim, now that I think about it, whoever shot at me didn't want to kill me, he only wanted to scare me or warn me. If he had wanted to kill me, he could have. He had a clear shot. And furthermore, why call the cops and tell them I had been shot at?

"I don't know Savannah, I just don't know. Listen; can you take me back to where this guy shot at you? I want to have a look around."

Jim and I took the dogs and headed back into the woods. I showed him where I was sitting and where the shooter was. After carefully examining the tree, Jim turned and looked at me.

"Okay Savannah, where's the bullet?" Jim's voice was filled with exasperation.

Damn. Busted. I fished the bullet out of my pocket, careful not to let him see I had the shell casings and handed it to him with a sheepish look on my face. Jim took the bullet, put it in his pocket and wordlessly walked out of the woods. I followed at a slower pace.

"I'm going to have a patrol car drive by your house regularly until I figure this thing out. Just promise me you'll be more careful and that you won't keep information from me any more." Jim's voice was stern.

"I promise. Now get out of here. I'll be fine."

Truth was I had an idea and I was dying to follow up on it. I led Jim to the door and waited until he was safely out of sight. I grabbed my purse and keys, checked all the doors and headed out.

I had noticed that the local flea market was having a gun and knife show this weekend, so after paying my 2 bucks; I parked my jeep and headed into the show. I wandered around until I found a gun dealer who was displaying a multitude of rifles and ammunition. I walked up to his booth and pulled the shell casings out of my pocket.

"Excuse me, can you tell me what kind of rifle these were shot out of?"

The man behind the booth paused and gave me the once over. He was a short, stocky man in his early 30's. His face was almost completely hidden by a long, brown beard and his hair was neatly pulled back into a long ponytail. He was dressed in a Harley T-shirt and there were tattoos plastered up and down his arms.

I became fascinated by a tattoo of a snake that wound its way around his right forearm, up his upper arm and disappeared under the sleeve of his shirt. When the muscles in his arm flexed, it looked as if the snake was crawling up his arm. I wondered where it ended up.

I have been told that there are some things a person is better off not knowing. I had a feeling this was one of those things.

It took a minute for me to realize he was talking to me. I snapped back into reality fast, but my eyes kept straying to the tattoo.

"Far as I can tell, it came from your typical Michigan hunting rifle, probably a 30/30. Something like this one." He motioned to a rifle lying on the table in front of him.

"Great. Thanks for your help." I said as he handed the casings back to me.

"Your FBI aren't you?" His question caught me off guard.

"Former. Why?" I responded cautiously.

"Andy Perkins. Former FBI. I saw you a couple of times at headquarters." He extended his hand as he spoke. We shook.

"I'm sorry, I don't remember you." It was true, I didn't.

"I looked different then. No tattoos. Shorter hair." He blushed as he spoke. "I heard about your partner. I'm sorry."

"Thanks. Why did you get out?" It wasn't often I had a chance to talk to someone from the Bureau.

"I got shot. They put me on disabled. Listen. I can get my wife to cover the booth for me for a while. Do you want to grab a coffee?"

I nodded in assent and we headed to the cafeteria and grabbed a cup of coffee.

The topic of the Robbie's murder soon crept into the conversation. Feeling like I could trust Andy, I laid the whole thing out for him. The murder scene, the symbols, the mystery man, everything. He listened intently, stopping me every once in a while to ask for clarification on one point or another. It didn't take long to realize that once you are FBI, you're always FBI.

As it turned out, Andy used to work in the section of the FBI that dealt with different cults. He was particularly interested in the symbols. We made arrangements to meet at my house in a few days. A fresh pair of eyes couldn't hurt.

I realized it was getting late so I said my good-byes and headed out of the show when I spotted the mystery man in the photograph. He was a few rows over looking at some rifles.

I started to head toward him, not letting him out of my sight, when I realized that Mrs. Maxwell was with him. She turned her head and spotted me. Despite my attempt to hide behind several men walking by. I saw her say something to the man. He turned and looked at me then they rapidly headed for the exit. I tried to follow them, but the show was pretty packed and I lost them in the crowd. Disappointed, I headed home.

Out of frustration, I spent the next few hours cleaning my house. Finally, out of hunger and exhaustion I decided to take a break. I made myself something to eat and headed into the den to check my e-mail.

My mailbox was pretty full. There were a few messages from some of my friends and the usual inquiries from police departments requesting my assistance and I spent over an hour reading and answering them. I then came upon a message from an address I didn't recognize. I clicked on the message to open it and was immediately sorry I did. The message read:

Savannah,

Saw your picture in the newspaper this morning. It didn't do you justice. Went for a walk in the woods today. Almost shot a doe, but then I remembered it wasn't doe hunting season. At least not yet.

It was unsigned, just like the first note. I recoiled away from the computer as if it had been a snake ready to strike. In a way it probably was. Damn it! What was with this guy? I flicked off the computer in disgust. After what seemed like an eternity, I left the den, poured a glass of wine and sat down to have a cigarette and think.

I was so lost in thought that it took me a couple of seconds to realize the phone was ringing. After a mad dash through the house to find the cordless, I answered it.

"Hey Savannah?" I didn't recognize the voice.

"Yes. This is Savannah." My voice sounded stronger than I felt.

"Hey, it's Bobby from the Stop Light. Listen, I think I may have found someone who knows something about that guy in the picture. Can you come up here and bring it with you?"

"I'm on the way." I hung up the phone and in less than one minute was out of the house and on my way to the Stop Light Tavern.

When I walked in, I saw Bobby and another man at the bar. Barb smiled and put a cold one up on the bar. I climbed up into the barstool and took a long swig of beer.

"Hey Savannah. This is Matt Winters." Bobby made the introductions and Matt and I shook hands.

Matt was tall and thin. I judged him to be about thirty or so. Despite his thin build, his arms boasted strong muscles. His skin was deeply tanned, and he had the hands of a hardworking man, thick with calluses.

"Bobby said you're looking for the man Tabby is seeing." His voice was deep with a slight Southern drawl.

"That's right." I responded and pulled the picture of Tabby and the mystery man out of my bag.

I handed it to Matt and he studied it carefully before handing it back to me. I waited with anticipation for him to speak.

"I've seen him. First name's Kenny. I don't know his last name. He came around the construction site Friday looking for work. I talked to him for a few minutes. He claimed to be a rougher. Said he's only been in town for a couple of weeks." He looked straight into my eyes when he spoke.

"A rougher?" I was thoroughly confused.

"Yeah, a rougher. You know, a guy who roughs in houses. But he wasn't."

"How do you know?"

"His hands. He didn't have the hands of a rougher. You see, a rougher will have callused hands, like mine," Matt held out his hands proudly. "I'm a rougher. See how my hands are all callused and rough? His were smooth. I know because I shook his hand."

When he held out his hands I noticed he was wearing an unusual ring. It was silver with a black and white cameo of a man on it.

"What a beautiful ring. Is it a family heirloom?" I asked as I took another sip of beer.

"It was my father's. My mother had it made for him for a wedding present." Matt looked fondly at the ring. "When my father died, my mother gave it to me. It is my most prized possession."

"So, where is the construction sight you are working at?" I said, as I motioned to Barb for another round.

"24 Mile and Sass. We're building houses. Do you know the area?"

"Yeah, I know where it is. It's right behind my house. Was Kenny hired?"

"I don't know. I told him to go up to the trailer to talk to the fore-man. I didn't see him after that." Matt took another long drink of beer.

Bobby spoke up. "So if this Kenny guy has only been in town for a couple of weeks, where did he meet Tabby?"

"I don't know Bobby. Does Tabby work?"

"She works at Flanders waiting tables. She probably met him there. It's that place on 23 Mile by the motel." Barb said. "My old man and I ate there three or four weeks ago and she was our waitress."

"Interesting." I turned to Matt. "Did you know Robbie?"

"Yeah, Robbie and I were working at the same site. He was a great guy. Hard worker too."

"Listen Matt, here's one of my cards. If Kenny shows up at the con-struction site, will you please give me call?"

Matt took my card and studied it carefully before putting it in his wallet. I spent another hour or so talking with everybody. By the time I left, it was well after midnight and I was exhausted.

I arrived home only to find Jim's Durango parked in front of my house. Not seeing anyone, I opened the front door to find Jim and the dogs sleeping soundly on the couch in the great room. I forgot Jim still had a key.

I shook Jim's foot as I walked into the kitchen, jarring him awake.

"Where in the hell have you been? Do you know what time it is?"

"Jim. Number one, you are not my father, husband, boyfriend or keeper. It is none of your business where I have been or what time I get in. What are you doing here anyway?" I was frustrated, tired and just wanted to go to bed.

"Don't get testy. I come bearing gifts." Jim opened his briefcase and pulled out a manila folder. "These are copies of the autopsy and crime scene reports. I thought you might want to see these." Jim tossed the folder on the coffee table.

I eagerly snatched up the folder and began to read. Jim casually walked to the front door.

"Call me if you want to discuss anything. See you later." With the same cold detachment that had broken us up, he strode out the door and locked it behind him.

The only real thing of interest was the fact that the car belonging to the Maxwell's had been wiped clean of prints. Everything else left at the scene was also free of prints. The report also confirmed my suspicion that the blood in the pentagram had come from the cat found in the dumpster.

I then turned my attention to the autopsy report. The cause of death had been a bullet to the back of the head at point blank range. No surprise there, but what was a surprise is that there were traces of a common poison in the bloodstream of Mr. Maxwell. The coroner determined that Mr. Maxwell had probably been unconscious when he was shot. So, the killer didn't want him to suffer. How nice. There was something rattling around in the back of my brain, just an inkling of a theory, but it just wouldn't come.

About 3:00 a.m. I locked the reports and Mr. Maxwell's file in my safe and decided to go to bed.

Sydney and Rambo wanted out, so I followed them out onto the deck. They scampered around the backyard, so I lit one more cigarette and sat down in a patio chair to think.

Rambo ran to the back fence and began to bark. I yelled at him to stop and that's when I noticed what he was barking at. There was a car parked a little ways down the road behind me in the area where the new subdivision was being built. I listened carefully and could make out the sound of an engine. It was too dark to make out any features of the car, but I saw a cigarette flame up when the driver took a drag. I quickly extinguished my cigarette and got the dogs to come in the house. I locked the doorwall, set the alarm and for the first time in two years, loaded my gun. I wouldn't be caught unawares this time.

CHAPTER 5

▼

A few days had passed and I still wasn't any closer to discovering what the symbols in the pentagram meant. I hadn't heard from Matt, so I assumed that Kenny hadn't been hired. That was a relief. I hadn't received any more mail from the killer and that had me worried. The more I could get him to communicate the better chance I had of forming a more accurate profile. The best I could do at this point was say that he was a male Caucasian, mid to late thirties, strong build, familiar with cults or satanic rituals and police procedures. He is highly intelligent with at least two or three years of college. Not much to go on, but it was a start.

The car that had been parked behind my house was still showing up with some regularity, but always late at night. It never stayed more than ten to fifteen minutes and consistently would turn its bright lights on the back of my house before backing down the road, turning around and heading out to Sass Road.

I hadn't talked to Jim since the funeral, but that was by his choice. I had introduced Jim and Ben to Bobby, Russ and Matt at the funeral and told him about them seeing Robbie the night he was murdered. Matt also told him about Kenny showing up at the construction site looking for work. Jim was really mad at me for not telling him sooner, but he'd get over it.

I got up early and let the dogs out. It had been a rough night. I had nightmares about Frank being killed and hearing that fatal shot over and over in my sleep. A man holding a rifle, dressed in fatigues kept passing in front of my eyes laughing cruelly. Tarot cards and the symbols in the pentagram had kept swimming in front of me, like looking through some eerie kaleidoscope, shrouding Frank's body, as he lay dead in his doorway. I had woken up more than once shaking and drenched in sweat.

I started a pot of coffee and then headed to the shower. I stood in the shower allowing the hot water to caress my body. It was having its effect. The nightmares were becoming a distant memory and I felt myself start to relax.

I stepped out of the shower feeling inspired or desperate, depending on your point of view. I had to decipher those symbols in the pentagram and made a mental note to call Andy Perkins.

I wrapped myself in a fluffy, warm towel and started toward the kitchen to get a cup of coffee. I was mid-way down the hall when I heard muted voices coming from the kitchen and Rambo barking furiously at the doorwall.

I quickly dashed back into my bedroom and grabbed my gun. I tiptoed down the hallway and peeked around the corner into the great room. It was empty. I saw Rambo and Sydney at the back door. They didn't look happy. I took a deep breath and darted across the great room until I got to the opening of the kitchen and dining area. Without hesitation I jumped into the kitchen, held my gun out in front of me and yelled, "Freeze".

Jim and Sandra were standing at the counter eating apple turnovers and drinking a cup of coffee. Sandra let out a hair raising shriek and tossed her apple turnover into the air. It promptly stuck to the ceiling. Without missing a beat, Jim looked over at me and said. "Cute towel, would you like a cup of coffee?"

The whole scene was ridiculous. If I hadn't been so mad, I probably would have laughed. I sat my gun down on the kitchen table and walked over to the doorwall to let in the dogs that were now barking wildly. They came charging through the door just in time to have the apple turnover fall from the ceiling onto the floor, which they promptly devoured in between giving Sandra and Jim a rowdy greeting.

I, on the other hand, came to the conclusion that way too many people had keys to my house. I wheeled around and faced both of them. Before I could speak, Jim handed me a cup of coffee and Sandra, who had finally recovered from her fright said, "Land sakes alive, Savannah, I swear you scared me half to death. Whatever possessed you charge into the kitchen with your gun drawn? What on earth were you thinking?!"

"What was I thinking?!" I slammed my cup of coffee down so hard it splattered all over the table. "Well, let's look at this shall we?" I felt myself winding up. "In the past two weeks I have had one of my clients murdered, been shot at, gotten threatening messages and have had mysterious cars show up in the middle of the night and park behind my house. So when I come out of the shower and hear voices in the house don't you think I have just a little cause for concern. Don't you people ever knock or ring the doorbell? What about the phone? Last time I checked it worked."

"Whoa, wait a minute." Jim, who had choked on his turnover during my dissertation, interjected, "What's this about threatening messages and your house being watched. Why didn't you tell me?" Jim ran his hands through his black curly hair in exasperation. His voice getting louder by the minute. "Damn it Savannah, this is serious. When are you going to learn you can't keep everything to yourself? I'm the lead detective on this case and I have a right to know what is going on. Last time I checked with the Chief, you hadn't returned any of his messages, nor have you officially joined the investigation. You keep this up and I'll have your private detective license pulled so fast it will make your head spin."

I was so mad I didn't even trust myself to speak. How dare he threaten me. Without a word I picked up my gun and walked back into my bedroom slamming the door behind me. I took my time getting dressed, hoping that they would be gone by the time I was finished. I headed into the bathroom to comb out my hair and brush my teeth.

I carefully appraised myself in the mirror. There wasn't much to appraise. I stood five-foot nothing and weighed ninety-five pounds. I made a mental note to get a haircut. My curly auburn hair was now down past my waist and definitely overpowering. I pulled my hair back into a ponytail and headed back into the kitchen to find Sandra sitting at the kitchen table waiting for me. She had a stern look in her eyes and I knew I was in for a good tongue-lashing. Something I really wasn't in the mood for.

I poured another cup of coffee and lit a cigarette. It didn't take long for Sandra to start in on me.

"You really blew it this time Savannah. Jim's really mad. Oh by the way, when you were in the shower some guy named Andy Perkins called. He left his number. I wrote it down on the pad by the phone."

"First of all Sandra," I responded as calmly as possible as I picked up the notepad with Andy's number on it. I tried to call Andy, but got his answering machine. I left him a message and then turned my attention back to Sandra. "I really don't care that Jim's mad. Granted, I probably should have told him about my house being watched, but I don't know if it's related to this case or another matter I'm working on. And until I'm sure, it's really none of his business. Second, I didn't tell him about the threatening messages because I didn't want to worry him. He has enough on his mind. Lastly, as much as I love seeing you, I really wish you would call first. It really did scare me to think someone was in my house. My God, Sandra, I could have shot you."

Someone had once said that the best defense is a good offense and that was the best I could come up with on such short notice.

Sandra looked up at me guiltily, "You're right. I'm sorry. I just didn't stop and think that it might scare you. Anyway, what are you up to today?" Sandra asked, rapidly steering the conversation elsewhere.

"Actually I was thinking about spending the day on the boat. Want to come?" I responded, letting her off the hook.

Sandra nodded her head in assent, as she stuffed another apple turnover in her mouth.

Sandra and I quickly cleaned up the kitchen, fed the dogs and headed to the marina.

When I was in the FBI, we had confiscated a boat from a big drug dealer in Florida. When the boat came up for auction, I bought it. It is a thirty-two foot Carver aft cabin, which is way too big for one person, but I fell in love with it. I have a passion for scuba diving, and although Lake St. Clair is shallow and somewhat murky, it is still fun to go diving in. I have made several trips on my boat into Lake Huron where the water is deep and the diving divine.

We got to the marina and were surprised to see that the new name, "Private Eyes". had been applied to the stern. It looked great.

We spent about an hour washing down the boat before navigating her out of the marina to the lake. The dark blue water was smooth, and sparkled like diamonds when the sun danced off the surface. We headed across Anchor Bay and dropped anchor about a mile offshore near Ashley. We spent most of the day relaxing and swimming in the warm water. My theory was that if I distanced myself from the case for awhile, I might come up with a fresh perspective. It didn't work.

We got home late in the afternoon and after Sandra left, I realized that I had forgotten to take the dogs for their usual Sunday morning romp through the woods. I changed into jeans, my favorite baggy T-shirt and hiking boots. I put the dogs on their leashes, grabbed my cell phone and headed out, tucking my gun into the waistband of my jeans. I wasn't going to take any chances this time.

We got to the edge of the woods and I let the dogs off their leashes and they happily raced off through the underbrush. I headed to the spot where I had been shot at. I wanted to have another look around.

I think it was the smell I noticed first. It was familiar. A sweet, sickly, smell that you never forget. It was the smell of death. I froze where I stood and carefully reached for my gun. Darting from tree to tree, I made my way closer toward the smell. I came to a small clearing and saw a large bundle tied to a tree. In front of the bundle was a large piece of cloth. It appeared to be a white sheet. It was held to the ground by four arrows, one in each corner. Painted on the sheet was a pentagram with different symbols than those left at the murder scene of Mr. Maxwell, drawn in blood.

Swallowing a scream, I released the safety off my gun and cautiously circled the area. After determining I was alone, I walked a little ways deeper into the woods and called the dogs. I wanted to keep them out the area. They came running up to me panting and out of breath. I noticed that they had blood on their paws, so after putting them back on their leashes and tying them to a tree, I headed in the direction they had come from.

I didn't have to go far. Lying about fifty feet away from the crime scene was a dead deer. Its gut had been slit open. That's where the blood from the pentagram had come from. I circled the deer, careful not to disturb any possible evidence. I then extended my circle out a little at a time. About twenty feet away from the deer I found a shell casing. It looked exactly the same as the casings left behind when I was shot at.

I headed back to the scene and dialed Jim on my cell phone. He answered in two rings.

"Jim Matthews."

"Jim, Its Savannah. I think our killer has struck again. I'm near the spot I was shot at in the woods. I think you and the team better get out here."

"We're on the way. Are you okay?" His voice was tense.

"I'm fine. I've got the dogs and my gun with me. I scouted out the area and I seem to be alone, at least for the moment. But hurry, okay?"

"I'll be right there. Be careful."

I sat down with the dogs, well away from the crime scene, to wait for Jim. It was only a matter of seconds before I heard the sirens pierce the eerie quiet of the woods. I got up and went to meet Jim. His partner, Ben was with him and I walked with them to the scene. I pointed out where the deer was so the crime scene unit could secure that area as well.

I borrowed a pencil and paper and carefully made a quick sketch of the pentagram and symbols.

The crime scene unit arrived and began processing the scene. A few minutes later Cal showed up with one of his technicians.

It took quite a while for the crime scene unit to process enough of the scene to allow us to get close to the bundle tied to the tree. After a short discussion, we decided that we didn't want to untie the knot because the type of knot a killer uses can provide valuable clues to his possible identity. We finally decided to cut the rope holding the body to the tree. Once that was done, Cal and his technician, Nick, laid the body carefully inside a body bag to preserve any evidence on the tarp. When they moved the body, a hand fell out of one side of the tarp. I recognized the ring on the hand. It was silver with a black and white cameo. I grabbed Ben who was standing next to me to steady myself and started to cry quietly. I knew who it was.

"Savannah, what is it?" Ben had wrapped his arms around me in a big bear hug.

"I know who it is." I said sobbing, "His name is Matt. I met him at the Stop Light Tavern. I recognize the ring. He is the one who told me about Kenny being at the construction site."

Jim had overheard our conversation and walked over to us. Wordlessly, he handed me his handkerchief and I took a few minutes to compose myself.

I walked over to Cal who was in the process of opening the tarp to expose Matt's body. Thrust into Matt's chest was a red-handled butterfly knife holding another tarot card.

I had spent most of last week studying the tarot book and knew that the card was the five of swords.

"What does it look like Cal?" Jim and Ben had come up behind me. It was Jim who had spoken. The closeness of his voice made me jump.

"From what I see so far, it looks the same as the first. Shot close range in the back of the head with a small caliber pistol. The knife was inserted shortly after death. The same as Mr. Maxwell. He's been here for awhile though, I would guess sometime last night, but I won't know more until I get him back to the morgue."

I nodded to Cal and walked away. I went over by the dogs and sat down on the ground. Jim came over a short while later.

"I don't like this Savannah. Two murders, probably by the same person this close together. That's an awful fast pace."

"I know Jim. I don't like it either." I looked up at him and saw the worried look on his face. "Jim, I was supposed to find the body. But I was supposed to find it this morning. Don't you see? The killer knows I always walk the dogs on Sunday mornings. Look at the facts. Two weeks ago I was shot at while walking the dogs through the woods. I didn't take the dogs for their usual walk through the woods this morning. I was late. Jim, the body was left here for my benefit. The killer is targeting me."

Jim digested this theory for a few minutes before speaking. "Then how do you explain Mr. Maxwell? You didn't find his body, an officer on patrol did."

"I can't explain it, but the only connection between Mr. Maxwell and Matt is that I knew them. Not well, but I had had recent contact with both of them and then a few days later they turn up dead."

"You might be right Savannah, and that scares me even more. Listen, I'm going to have an officer take you and the dogs home and stay there until we're finished here. I'll stop by later. Be careful and stay put." Jim said firmly.

I didn't want to leave. But I was too weak to argue. I obediently untied the dogs from the tree and followed Jim out of the woods. Jim packed us into a patrol car and we went home.

I immediately dismissed the officer who brought me home. He had better things to do with his time then baby-sit me. I checked my messages. Mr. Walker had called and said he was leaving to go out of town in the morning. I made a note to follow Mrs. Walker the following night, then poured a big glass of wine and headed into the den.

I grabbed the tarot card book off my desk and looked up the five of swords. It had been right side up so it would be interpreted as meaning failure, defeat, degradation or conquest by unfair means over others. Cowardliness, cruelty, malice.

That made sense. If Matt had been poisoned like Mr. Maxwell that would render him helpless to defend himself. So to the killer it would be a conquest by unfair means. It certainly reeked of cowardliness and cruelty.

I then turned my attention to the symbols in the pentagram. They were totally different than the symbols left at Mr. Maxwell's murder. Back to square one.

I knew I had to tell the gang at the Stop Light Tavern myself. I didn't want them to hear it on the news, so I grabbed my car keys and headed out.

I arrived at the Stop Street Tavern and sat in the car for a few minutes trying to figure out how I was going to break the news about Matt to the gang. With a long face and a heavy heart, I got out of my car and headed for the door. Bobby, Russ and Barb shouted their greetings as I entered. I slid into a barstool and gratefully took a long swig of the beer Barb sat down in front of me. After taking a deep breath, I turned to face Bobby and Russ.

"Listen guys, I have some bad news." I felt my eyes welling up with tears. The shock of the day finally sinking in. "Matt was found murdered this afternoon. It is my belief that he was killed by the same person that killed Mr. Maxwell." I said that all in one breath, not daring to stop. Tears were rolling down my cheeks as I looked at Bobby and Russ.

Bobby reached out and wrapped me in a huge hug. While I sobbed against his shoulder, I felt like I was being smothered. Pulling myself away, I grabbed a napkin and wiped my eyes.

"Who found him?" Bobby asked quietly.

"I did." I responded. There was nothing else to say.

"How did he die?" Barb, wiping her eyes asked me.

"Not that it's much consolation, I don't think he suffered. I won't know for sure until the autopsy results are in. I'm sorry you guys. I never saw this coming. I'm just so sorry." I was starting to cry again. I felt as though I had let down all of them.

"It's not your fault, Savannah." Bobby said as he handed me his handkerchief. "You had no way of knowing that this was going to happen."

Bobby looked at Russ. "We should go over to Matt's house. His mother could probably use some company."

Russ nodded his assent and then turned to me, "Are you going to be okay Savannah? Why don't you let us drive you home."

"I'll be okay. You guys go ahead. I'm going to head home myself." I slid off the barstool and looked at them. "I promise you I will find out who did this." I said with newfound determination.

"We know you will." Bobby responded. "Keep in touch."

They walked me out to my jeep. We all hugged and said goodbye. I started up the jeep and with a small wave, headed out of the parking lot to go home.

I pulled up to find a patrol car stationed in front of my house. I hit the garage door opener and waved at the policeman as I pulled in the garage. I shut the door behind me and made my way into the house.

After pouring myself a glass of wine, I let the dogs out and followed them out onto the deck. There was no sign of the car that had been staking out my house, so I called the dogs and headed back inside. I noticed the light on my answering machine blinking so I hit the button to replay the messages.

"Hi Savannah. This is Chief Briggs. I would like to see you in my office at nine tomorrow morning. Sharp."

I saluted the phone and uttered a sarcastic, "Yes Sir!" I gulped down my glass of wine and after carefully checking all the doors; I set the alarm and headed to bed. It had been a long day.

I wandered into my bathroom to take a quick shower. I looked like hell. My face was puffy and my eyes were red and swollen from crying. I got out of the shower, slipped into a pair of lavender sweats and got into bed.

Rambo and Sydney sensing that something was wrong leapt up onto the bed and settled in next to me. I was just dozing off when I heard the alarm go off on the house. Instantly awake, I grabbed my gun and warily headed down the hallway to the front door. I was halfway down the hall when I heard Jim. "Damn it Savannah. I forgot the code."

I lowered my gun and walked into the foyer. I entered the access code and the alarm fell silent. I wish I could say the same for Jim. He turned on me like a mad dog.

"Where in the hell did you go? What were you thinking? I had a car out there watching an empty house! Why is it that you can't just stay put? Damn it Savannah this has got to stop!" While Jim was yelling at me, his face turned beet red and a vein was standing out on his fore-head. Perhaps I had pushed it just a little bit too far this time.

"I'm sorry." I said meekly. "I went up to the Stop Street Tavern to tell Bobby and Russ about Matt. I thought it would be easier if they heard it from me." My response seemed to satisfy him because he calmed down and promptly changed the subject.

"I just came from the station. The Chief wants to talk to you. Tomorrow."

"I know. He left a message on my answering machine. Why me? I'm sure if he asked the FBI would send in a profiler."

"I told him that you had found the body. I also told him that Matt and you were acquaintances. He doesn't blame you Savannah. He is just concerned that lately everybody you come in contact with gets themselves murdered." I could tell by the look on Jim's face that he wished he could take back his last sentence.

"God Savannah. I'm sorry. I didn't mean that the way it sounded. It's just that I am so damn frustrated. With all the clues left at the scene, you think we would be closer to finding out who was doing this." He had gotten up and started to pace the room.

"I know, Jim. By the way, I looked up the tarot card. It's the five of swords. It means that the killer made his conquest by unfair means. My best guess is that Matt was poisoned like Mr. Maxwell. The card also possibly means that the killings were cruel and the act of a coward. Like we couldn't figure out that by ourselves. I haven't been able to decipher the symbols left in the pentagrams yet. It all seems familiar somehow, but I just can't figure out why."

There it was again. That nagging faint sense of déjà vu; a distant memory attempting to claw its way up to the surface, but not quite being able to make it. Damn, I hate when that happens.

I walked into the kitchen to pour myself another glass of wine and grabbed my cigarettes. As I was leaving the kitchen, I noticed that the light was blinking on my answering machine. Someone must have called while I was in the shower. I hit the button.

"Hi Savannah, it's Andy. Give me a call. Talk to you later."

Jim and I looked at each other. I waited for the next message.

A mechanically altered tin sounding voice echoed through the room, "Savannah, did you find the present I left you in the woods? You really should be more selective about who you associate with."

I quickly grabbed the cordless phone and checked the caller-id. Andy's number was there, but the second phone call had just registered as "Private". I slammed the phone back into its base in disgust.

"Damn it Savannah. This guy's sick. You're not safe here. I want you to pack a bag and go to Sandra's for awhile. Just lay low until I can figure this thing out." Jim was pacing the kitchen furiously.

Calmly, I opened the cupboard and took out a big shot glass and poured Jim a double shot of scotch. I looked into his eyes as I handed him his drink and for the first time since I'd known him, I saw fear.

"Jim. I am not going anywhere. I'm perfectly safe here. I've got the alarm system, the dogs and my gun. Besides, I'm the only link to the killer we have. I'm afraid that if I disappear, he will accelerate his killing agenda. I don't think he is out to kill me, at least not yet. This is all a game to him and I don't think he's through playing."

Jim finished his drink in one big gulp and reached for the bottle of scotch. He poured himself another one before turning back to me.

"Why do you have to be so damn stubborn? Why can't you just once do what I ask without having to argue with me?" Jim took a sip of his drink. I took advantage of the silence to respond.

"Because I'm right and you know it. Look. We're both just frustrated and tired. Go home, get some rest and I'll talk to you in the morning. Don't worry. I'll be fine." I kept my voice calm and gentle. You kill more bees with honey than vinegar.

Jim reached out and popped the tape out of the answering machine. "I'm taking this tape in for analysis. Maybe the tech boys can come up with something. Do you have a spare tape?"

I motioned to the drawer on his right.

"By the way," Jim asked as he opened the drawer and inserted a clean tape into the machine, "Who's Andy?"

"He's ex-FBI. He worked in the cult division. I'm hoping that he will be able to decipher the symbols left in the pentagrams."

"Good idea." Jim nodded his head in approval. "Let me know if you come up with anything. Don't forget your meeting with the Chief in the morning."

"I won't." I responded as I led him to the door. After we said our good-byes, I locked the door, set the alarm, checked to make sure my gun was loaded and headed back to bed.

CHAPTER 6

---▼---

I hated getting called into the Chief's office. I always felt like I had done something wrong. Maybe it was a throwback to my school days when I got called down to the principal's office. I always did have a problem with authority figures.

I got out of the shower, got dressed and wandered out into the driveway to find my morning paper, which was always an adventure into the unknown. It had ended up in the row of hedges that line both sides of my driveway. I reached into the hedge to retrieve it and got stuck by about a dozen thorns. I made a mental note to take out the hedges.

I walked back into the house, made my way to the kitchen and poured a cup of coffee. As I was taking my first sip, I flipped open the paper. Matt's murder was all over the front page. Tossing the paper aside, I gulped my coffee, called in the dogs and headed out to my mechanic's place to have an automatic starting system installed in my jeep. I dropped off the truck, and Phil, my mechanic, gave me a lift to the police station. I would get Jim to drive me home.

The police station is a converted three-story house in the middle of town. It is neatly landscaped and really quite pretty. The outside has been completely renovated and is painted a crisp, clean, white trimmed in navy blue gingerbread. It might look pretty on the outside, but the inside is all business.

With a heavy sigh, I said goodbye to Phil and headed in. I gave my name to the desk sergeant and he called the Chief to let him know I was waiting.

I settled myself into a chair and picked up the magazine lying on the table next to me. I was deeply engrossed in an article about the plight of the sea bass when I heard a deep rumbling coming from the end of the hallway.

I turned my head and saw Chief Briggs heading down the hall. The Chief is a six foot five, three hundred fifty-pound man who bears a strong resemblance to a Sherman tank, and has about as much tact. His deep-set, hazel eyes darted from side to side as he rolled down the hallway taking in every detail. His reddish brown hair was neatly trimmed military style and his blue uniform was freshly pressed.

I tossed the magazine back on the table and stood up as he approached.

"Savannah. How nice of you to make it, and on time." His sarcasm wasn't lost on me.

"Chief Briggs," I responded sweetly with my best smile, "so nice of you to make the time to see me."

"I thought we would meet in the conference room. It's more comfortable in there. Would you care for some coffee?" He asked, just as sweetly.

"No, thank you." I had tasted the coffee at the police station before. An experience I was not ready to repeat.

We headed into the conference room. Jim was already there. I had been set up.

"I hope you don't mind, but I've asked Jim to join us." Chief Briggs smiled broadly as he spoke. He loved to keep people just slightly off center and I could tell he was enjoying this immensely.

"No, of course not," I replied keeping my voice calm and even. I would not let the Chief get the best of me.

"The reason I called this meeting, Savannah," The Chief began, motioning me into a chair, "is to ask you to formally join the investigation in the capacity of a profiler. I am aware that you have a connection to the two men who have been murdered and that the killer has made contact with you on at least two occasions. You will be paid the normal rate and be expected to share any information you find with Jim and the rest of the team assigned to this matter. In return, we will share all the information we have gathered. Sound fair?"

I glanced over at Jim who was leaning back in his chair with an amused smirk on his face. He too loved to watch me squirm.

I felt like a trapped rat. If I accepted the assignment, I would have to work under the structure of the police department. If I turned down the assignment, Jim could turn my investigation into a living hell. Carefully contemplating the Chief's words I formulated a response. There was a loophole, a tiny one, but a loophole nevertheless.

"I accept your offer to join the team as a profiler. My duties will be that of a profiler only. Is that clear?" I glanced around the table as I finished.

The Chief was wearing the smile of a Cheshire cat. He thought he had won. Jim was looking at me through narrowed eyes. He knew I was up to something, but he wasn't quite sure what.

"Perfectly clear, Savannah." The Chief said, rising from his chair to shake my hand. "Welcome aboard. I will make the proper arrangements within the department for you to have complete access to all information we have on the case."

"Thank you," I responded with a slight smile, remembering the copy of Mr. Mathew's murder investigation file safely tucked away in my safe, "Now, if there's nothing else, I have some other cases I have to close out so I can devote my time to the investigation. Jim, could you please give me a lift to Phil's Gas Station so I can pick up my jeep?"

"No problem. Let's go." Jim replied as he rose from the chair.

We said goodbye to the Chief and headed out to Jim's Durango. We rode in silence until we were almost to Phil's. Finally, Jim spoke up.

"What exactly are you up to Savannah?" He asked suspiciously.

"What exactly are you talking about, Jim?" I snapped back, knowing full well what he meant.

"You gave into the Chief way to easy. I know you have an angle. I'm just not sure what it is yet. So why don't you explain it to me so we can both save a lot of time." Jim responded.

"I didn't have a choice but to give in to the Chief." I said, "If I didn't join the investigation you would make my life a living hell. If I joined the investigation you would still make my life a living hell, but to a lesser degree. It was simply a matter of deciding how much hell I wanted to put up with."

"How can you even say that?" Jim said with a shocked tone to his voice and that hurt little boy look in his Paul Newman eyes. He opened his mouth to add something, but I cut him off at the pass.

"How can I say that!" I responded, trying to keep my voice and my anger in check, "I'll tell you exactly how I can say that. Who was it that threatened to have my private detective license pulled? Who is it that keeps showing up at my house unannounced and, may I add, uninvited? Now you can't pull my license because the Chief won't let you and at least now when you come by the house you might have a good reason. That's how I can say that."

As I finished, we pulled into Phil's Gas Station and I leapt from the truck and had almost made a clean get away, bur Jim stopped me before I made it past the hood of the truck.

"Savannah, you know I would never have your license pulled. I was just angry and scared. I don't know what I would do if something ever happened to you. I just want you to be safe and happy." Jim's voice was as soft as a caress as he gave me a hug. I could feel the warmth of his body and smell the intoxicating aroma of his Pierre Cardin cologne.

I could not allow myself to give in. I couldn't afford the emotional cost. I wrestled myself out of his arms and looked up into his eyes.

"You should have thought of that before you walked out on me. I have to go." I responded quietly as I turned away and headed toward the door, angry with myself for reacting so harshly.

I paid Phil, and after brief instructions on how the freshly installed auto-start worked, headed home.

I let the dogs out and headed into the den to check my e-mail and pull Mr. Walker's file to plan my activities for tonight.

My e-mail proved to be uneventful, so after carefully reviewing Mr. Walker's file I tucked it in my brief case, corralled the dogs back inside, set the alarm and headed out. I had other errands to attend to today.

I decided I couldn't avoid the inevitable, so I swung by Matt's mother's house. I pulled into the driveway of a modest, but well-kept colonial. I rang the doorbell and an attractive woman in her mid to late fifties opened the door.

"Hi, I'm Savannah Williams. I was.." I started.

"Oh, Ms. Williams, I'm so glad you stopped by. Detective Matthews mentioned that you were the one who found Matt's body. Please come in. I'm Helen Winters, Matt's mom." She said and stood aside to allow me to enter.

Grace and class under pressure, I was impressed.

"I'm so sorry about Matt. Is there anything I can do?" I asked politely as I settled myself into a muted floral print couch. Helen settled herself in a matching overstuffed chair across from me.

"Yes," Helen replied quietly, but with conviction. "Find out who did this to my son."

"I will, Mrs. Winters. I promise you that." I answered with equal conviction. "Would you mind if I asked you a couple of questions? It would help me a lot in the investigation."

"What would you like to know dear? Oh my, I forgot my manners, may I get you something to eat or drink?" Helen asked, flustered that her manners had slipped.

"Not unless you are going to have something? How about if you rest and I go into the kitchen and make us some tea?" I asked, rising from the couch. It was the only polite thing to do, plus I never missed an opportunity to snoop.

"That would be so nice of you dear." Helen replied gratefully. "I just can't seem to get it together since Matt died. You know how it is."

"I'll just be a minute." I responded and headed into the kitchen.

Helen Winter's kitchen was just off the living room to the left. It was a big, bright country kitchen decorated cheerfully in shades of yellows and blues. A café table adorned with a yellow and white checked gingham tablecloth and two chairs with matching seat cushions were tucked into an octagon shaped eating area with floor to ceiling windows. There was tons of counter space and a baker's rack with bright copper pots and pans hung from the ceiling over the snack bar.

I found a yellow teakettle on the counter and after filling it with fresh water set it on the stove to boil. It took me several attempts to find the cups and saucers, which were a blue and white speckled pattern and matched perfectly with the country atmosphere of the room. White and blue checked canisters adorned one area of the counter next to the sink and I pulled out two tea bags. In the cabinet next to the mugs I found a cream and sugar set and filled the creamer up with fresh milk from the refrigerator. There was little else to see, so I poured the water into the cups, added the tea bags and headed back into the living room. I set the cups down on the coffee table and trotted back into the kitchen to retrieve the cream and sugar and two spoons.

Helen carefully added two sugar cubes to her tea, stirred it, and sat back in her chair, gratefully sipping her tea. I on the other hand added four cubes of sugar and a good supply of milk to my cup. I hated tea.

"This is so nice dear. Thank you." Helen said. "Now what did you want to know?"

"Well, where was Matt the day of the murder?" I decided to begin slowly and work my way up to the real point of my visit.

"Let me think for minute." Helen said, putting her index finger to her lips. "Saturday night he called and left a message on the answering machine saying he was spending the night at Bobby's. They were up at the Stop Light. He said that he was going to work on Sunday. He got double time on Sunday and he was saving to buy a new truck. He never came home." Helen became choked up as she spoke and a lone tear trickled down her cheek that was quickly brushed away. I could tell her son was the light of her life. I felt miserable.

"Mrs. Winter's," I began carefully, giving her a couple of seconds to compose herself, "did Matt receive any unusual mail a couple of days before he died?"

"I really didn't pay any attention to the mail the last few days. Saturday morning into late afternoon I was busy setting up for the woman's club auction at the VFW hall in town. I remember I got home around four thirty, heard Matt's message on the machine, showered and changed and then went back to the VFW hall to run the auction. It didn't end until well after midnight. You know how those things go. I got home and fell into bed. Sunday morning I had to be back at the VFW hall to help clean up. The mail is on the desk." Helen said motioning toward an antique mahogany roll-top desk majestically sitting in one corner of the living room. "You are welcome to look."

I walked over to the desk and looked at the pile of mail neatly stacked on the desk. I immediately discarded the small, letter size envelopes and dug through the pile to the large brown envelope at the bottom of the stack. Without touching the envelope, I could see that there was no return address and the envelope had a computer printed white label addressed to Matt Winters. It was postmarked Mt. Clements and had been mailed Thursday. It probably had been delivered Saturday. Jackpot!

"Mrs. Winters," I began cautiously, "there is an envelope here addressed to Matt that I believe is from the killer. I'm going to have to call one of the detectives to come over here with an evidence kit. Is that okay?"

"Of course it is. What envelope? Why would the killer send Matt mail? Helen asked, thoroughly confused and slightly agitated.

I explained to her that the killer's first victim had received a tarot card in the mail a couple of days before he was murdered and that I believed that this envelope contained a tarot card as well. Mrs. Winters nodded her understanding, and then added "Call whoever you need to. I'll do anything to help. Why didn't the police ask me about the mail?"

"Probably because they weren't looking for it." I responded quietly.

Excitedly, I picked the phone up off the desk and began to dial. Midway through dialing I set the phone back in to the receiver. I realized that I would have to call Jim to bring me an evidence kit and after the fight we just had, this was not something I relished doing.

In a flash of inspiration, I picked the phone back up and dialed the Ashley Police Department. The desk sergeant answered and I asked for Ben Mills. I could deal with Jim's partner a lot easier than I could deal with Jim.

"Ben Mills." Ben said as he picked up the phone.

"Hi Ben, its Savannah. I'm at the Winter's house. I need you to come over here with an evidence kit as soon as possible." I said as professionally as I could muster, but I could feel my heart beating against my chest.

"Sure Savannah," Ben said, catching my enthusiasm. "What's up?"

"There is a large brown envelope addressed to Matt. I think it's from the killer. Probably another tarot card, but I can't be sure until I open it and I don't have the proper equipment with me." I answered.

"On my way. I'll call Jim and have him meet me there." Ben replied.

"No!" I said rather loudly. Lowering my voice I continued, "Jim and I had a fight when he dropped me off to get my jeep. Call him after I leave. I really don't want to see him right now."

"Whatever you say." Ben said with a slight laugh to his voice. "I'll be there in a couple of minutes. Bye."

I waited for what seemed like an hour, but was more like ten minutes before Ben showed up with a portable evidence kit. I led him into the living room and over to the desk. He sat the evidence kit, which resembled a large fishing tackle box, down on the floor and carefully scrutinized the envelope without touching it. While he was doing that, I knelt down and opened the evidence kit. It contained all the normal stuff, plastic bags of various sizes, latex gloves, red evidence tape, fingerprint kit, tweezers, small exacto knives and other assorted goodies.

I donned a pair of latex gloves and picked up an exacto knife. Ben reached into the kit and pulled out an appropriate sized plastic bag and red evidence tape. Carefully, I slit open the bottom of the envelope. I didn't want to open it from the top because that could destroy valuable DNA evidence if the killer licked the envelope to seal it.

Ben and I worked in silence, but I could feel the tension mount as we got closer to discovering the contents of the envelope. Once I slit open the bottom of the envelope, Ben took the exacto knife from my hand and wordlessly handed me a pair of tweezers.

Taking the tweezers, I carefully reached into the envelope to fish out the contents. I slid a piece of cardboard halfway out and then gingerly slid it the rest of the way careful to only handle the very edges.

Glued to the piece of cardboard was a tarot card. It was the Two of Wands. Ben and I examined the card for a couple of minutes before I carefully dropped it into the evidence bag Ben held open for me. We then sealed the envelope in another bag. Ben took the red evidence tape and sealed both bags and then placed them into the evidence kit. They would be taken to the lab for testing.

"Any ideas?" Ben asked, as he carefully repacked the evidence kit and closed it.

"Not yet, but at least the killer hasn't changed his pattern." I responded. "I'm going home in a few minutes to pick up the tarot card book. Call Jim and I'll meet you guys up at the station in about twenty minutes."

Ben was explaining to Mrs. Winters what had happened and what was going to be done next. He also asked to take her fingerprints so that they could be identified on the envelope. She readily agreed.

While Ben was taking Mrs. Winter's fingerprints, I took the empty cups and saucers into the kitchen, rinsed them out and put them in the dishwasher, then rejoined Ben and Mrs. Winters in the living room. Ben rose as I entered.

"Ready Savannah?" He asked.

"All set." I replied.

We promised to keep Mrs. Winters informed of any new developments and headed out to our cars.

I headed home, let the dogs out and headed for the den to check out the tarot card.

I found the Two of Wands in the tarot card book. The card showed a man looking out over the ocean; he has a globe in one hand and a long staff in the other. Another staff is in a ring on the other side of the man. Roses and lilies are formed in the shape of crosses on the left side of the card.

I remembered that the card was glued upside down on the cardboard, so I looked at the definition of a reversed card. It meant physical suffering, sadness, domination by others. Our killer was becoming bolder, gaining confidence. This was not good.

I let the dogs in, gave them a treat, and after tucking the book into my briefcase, headed out to the police station.

Ben and Jim were already waiting for me in the conference room when I arrived. Ben gave me a friendly greeting, Jim didn't. The best he could muster was a small smile through gritted teeth.

I sat down at the table and opened my briefcase. I took out the tarot card book and read them the description and meaning. I also gave them my impressions that the killer was gaining confidence and would perhaps become bolder.

Ben handed me a copy of Matt's file and I took a few minutes to review them. The autopsy results showed that he had died in the same manner as Mr. Maxwell. Shot in the back of the head execution style. His blood work revealed that he had been poisoned with the same poison as Mr. Maxwell. The tarp didn't reveal any trace evidence except that which had been at the scene and had probably been new when used to wrap Matt's body in.

I then turned my attention to the ballistics report. The test showed that the same gun had been used to kill both Mr. Maxwell and Matt. A hunting rifle had shot the deer and no shell casings had been found at the scene. There was no way to tell if it was the same rifle that had been used to shoot at me in the woods. The bullet had been removed from the deer when it had been gutted.

I closed the files and looked up at Jim and Ben who had been waiting patiently as I read through the reports.

"Okay. Where do we stand?" I asked, looking at both of them.

Jim was the first to speak, "I went up to the Stop Light last night to talk to Bobby and Russ. They won't talk to me. They said that they are willing to help out in any way they can but that they will only talk to you. They kept saying that they want nothing to do with the man that broke Savannah's heart. Gees, Savannah, what did you tell them?"

"I didn't tell them anything!" I responded defensively. Regaining my composure, I continued, "Jim, this is a small town, everybody knows everybody and everybody knows everybody's business. It is common knowledge around town that you walked out on me. They could have heard it anywhere. You know that. You've lived here long enough."

"Okay kids," Ben interjected, "let's keep this civil. Savannah, can you get in touch with Bobby and Russ and talk to them tonight?"

"I have another case I'm working on tonight, but it should wrap up relatively early. I'll go by the Stop Light on my way home and talk to them if they are there." I answered. I was rather bothered by the fact that neither Bobby nor Russ had mentioned seeing Matt before he was murdered.

Changing the subject, I asked, "Have you guys gotten a handle on Kenny or Mrs. Maxwell yet?"

"We've had people watching the Maxwell house." Ben said, he went on to elaborate, "Mrs. Maxwell is living there alone as far as we can tell.

She goes to work and comes home. Once a week she goes to her mother's house up in Richmond. There has been no sign of Kenny. We think he is still around, we just don't know where. Mrs. Maxwell gave us the slip a few days ago so she might have met with him then. She knows she is being watched, so she's going to be careful. I'm thinking of pulling back a little bit to see if he shows up."

"That's probably a good idea. Although there is a chance that they aren't seeing each other anymore." I responded.

"Have you met with that Andy guy to see if he can decipher the symbols yet?" Jim asked.

"We keep missing each other. I am going to call him later and see if I can set up an appointment for sometime tomorrow though. I know I've seen symbols like that before. I just can't remember when." Frustration crept into my voice as I responded.

"Who's Andy?" Ben asked, perplexed.

"Andy is some guy she met at the flea market," Jim answered, "he's ex-FBI and is familiar with cults and satanic groups. Savannah thinks he might be able to help."

"I hope so," Ben replied, "we really could use a break in this one. The killer is not leaving much to work with. He's quite good at what he does."

We discussed a few other small items, and I stopped by the Crime Lab to check out an evidence kit. By the time I got out of there it was late afternoon. After a trip to the grocery store and the post office to check my box and went home.

The dogs greeted me wildly. They love shopping day. They know I always bring them a treat. I pulled two huge soup bones out of the bag and put them in a pot to boil while I sorted through the rest of the groceries.

I drained the bones, ran them under cold water to cool them off and gave them to the dogs to munch on while I went through my mail.

I got the usual bills, junk mail and letters from other police agencies asking for help or advice on certain matters as well as several payments for cases I had worked on. There was nothing from the killer.

Setting aside the mail, I called Andy and left a message and then went into my bedroom to take a shower and change before I headed out to follow Mrs. Walker.

I stood in the shower allowing the hot water to do its job. It was having its effect and I felt myself start to relax.

"Is this a private party or can anyone join in?" A deep voice boomed, echoing off the bathroom walls.

After almost jumping out of my skin. I let out a piercing scream and peeked out of the shower to find Jim leaning against the wall of the bathroom with a slight grin on his face. Turning off the water, I quickly grabbed a towel and wrapped myself up. When I trusted myself to speak, I looked up at him.

"Just who in the hell do you think you are bursting into my bathroom like that? Give me my key to the house right now!" I held out my hand as I spoke.

"Sorry. I just couldn't resist" Jim was doubled over in a fit of laughter. "If you could have seen your face." He casually sauntered out of the bathroom and headed into my bedroom still chuckling.

I had no choice but to follow. Besides, I was getting cold.

Jim sprawled out on my bed and was immediately joined by Sydney and Rambo, along with their bones. I, on the other hand, stomped around my bedroom gathering the articles of clothing I wanted to wear tonight.

Without a word to Jim, I walked back into my bathroom and slammed the door. I could hear him laugh on the other side of my door. I made a mental note to call a locksmith and have the locks changed. Enough was enough.

I took my time dressing. I decided to wear a pair of black jeans, a black T-shirt and black tennis shoes. If I had to go traipsing around in the dark after Mrs. Walker, I wanted to be able to blend into the shadows.

I combed my hair, brushed my teeth, put on a little make-up and emerged from the bathroom still angry with Jim.

"Did you come over here for a reason, or do you make it a habit of showing up in women's bathrooms unannounced?" I asked sarcastically.

"Actually," Jim replied, trying to control another wave of laughter, "I stopped by to see if you needed any help tonight. Besides, maybe if Bobby and Russ see us together, they will be more likely to talk to me in the future."

"I knew there was an ulterior motive. You didn't come by to see what you could do for me, you came by because you need me to do something for you." I snapped. "Sorry, but I work alone now. Please leave." I said, pointing toward my bedroom door.

Reluctantly Jim got off the bed, scratched the dogs behind the ears and walked out the front door without a word. The more things change, the more they stay the same.

CHAPTER 7

▼

I waited until Jim was safely out of sight then checked my stakeout bag and left.

There are many things that are vital to a successful stakeout. A good camera equipped with a night vision lens, night vision goggles, cell phone, pad of paper, pen and a watch. But perhaps the most vital ingredient in a successful stakeout is to drive through Mc Donald's on the way to your destination. With my Double Quarter Pounder and cheese, fries and diet coke stowed away, I headed over to the Walkers'.

Mr. & Mrs. Walker live in a refurbished white clapboard house with a covered porch that gracefully wraps around the front of the house. Two lavender wicker rockers and small matching table reside on the porch along with an old-fashioned porch swing. Hanging baskets overflowing with plants complete the country look. Their house is located on a dirt road out in the middle of nowhere. I had driven by the house a couple of days ago so I was familiar with the layout. A quick glance out the window as I drove by revealed that Mrs. Walker's blue minivan was in the driveway. I had also learned that there was an abandoned farmhouse about an eighth of a mile down the road and across the street.

I carefully backed into the driveway of the old farmhouse and cut my lights. I rolled down the windows of my jeep and settled in. It could be a long wait.

As I munched on my Quarter Pounder, I started thinking about Mr. Maxwell and Matt's murders. We had to come up with something soon. The press was having a field day with the lack of progress. I wasn't getting any closer to solving the symbols in the pentagram and I knew that the killer was out there planning his next move. My job was to anticipate that move and block it, not an easy task.

I became so lost in thought that it took a few seconds for the sound of tires on gravel to register. I looked toward the Walkers' and saw the minivan backing out of the driveway and head down the road. I waited a couple of seconds before easing the jeep out the driveway, and without turning on my lights, slowly followed.

Once Mrs. Walker turned on the main road toward town, I hit my lights and pulled out after her.

I glanced in my rearview mirror and saw a car pull out behind me, turning his lights on when he hit the main road. What was up with this? I wondered and more importantly, where did he come from and who was he?

Great, the tail picked up a tail. Now I had a decision to make. Did I give up following Mrs. Walker and ditch the tail, or did I continue on. I decided to continue. Nothing ventured nothing gained.

Mrs. Walker headed through town and toward Algonac. After driving for about thirty minutes, Mrs. Walker turned into a restaurant called the Fisherman's Bar and Grill. I pulled in and parked. The car that had been following me pulled in the parking lot of the bait store across the street, turned around and headed back into town. It was too dark to see what type of car it was. The only thing I could ascertain is that there was one occupant, probably a man.

When I turned back around, I caught a glimpse of Mrs. Walker entering the bar. I waited until she had been inside a few minutes then entered the bar.

The Fisherman's Bar & Grill was pretty much what I expected. It had an open floor plan and was decorated in various shades of dark green and burgundy, with various fishing items displayed throughout. I found a seat at the bar and ordered a glass of wine. I flipped the bartender a five and as I took my first sip of wine, swiveled my barstool around and scanned the room for Mrs. Walker. I finally spotted her at a cozy table for two talking intently to an attractive, well-built blonde hair, blue-eyed man. I watched them chat for about an hour before they got up and headed for the door. I followed a few seconds later.

When I got to my jeep I noticed that Mrs. Walker and the blonde man had stopped in the parking lot to chat. I grabbed my camera and snapped off a few pictures. The blond man headed back into the bar and Mrs. Walker got into her car and headed back to her house. After watching her house for about an hour, I decided that the blonde man wasn't going to show, so I headed up to the Stop Light Tavern.

Bobby and Russ were at the bar when I walked in. After we exchanged greetings, I ordered a glass of wine and lit up a cigarette. I wasn't sure how I wanted to begin.

"Savannah," Bobby said with a sheepish look on his face, "Russ and I have something to tell you and you're going to be real sore at us, but we didn't think it was important at the time."

"I'm listening." I responded evenly.

"Well, you see, it's like this." Bobby began, pausing for a big swig of beer before continuing, "Matt was with us the night before he was murdered. I know we should have told you, but you were so upset when you came up here to tell us about Matt, that we just couldn't. We're sorry Savannah, we really are."

Bobby finished and looked at me with a pleading look in his eyes.

"I know Bobby, Mrs. Winters told me when I saw her today." I said quietly, "So, why don't you tell me about it now."

"Well, Matt, Russ and I met here after work. It got late and Matt had had a lot to drink, so I told him to call his mom and tell her he was spending the night at my place. About one o'clock we were ready to leave. Matt had quit drinking about an hour before that and had switched to coffee. He said he was feeling better and that he would just go home. Matt said it was just easier if he went home because he had to put some tools in his truck for the job the next day."

"That's it?" I asked.

"Yes," Bobby said, relieved that he had lifted that burden from his mind, "Please don't be mad Savannah."

"I'm not mad." I replied, "So now do you want to explain to me why you wouldn't talk to Jim, I mean Detective Matthews?" I asked, not quite letting them off the hook yet.

"Well, it's like this." Bobby began, "The talk around town is that Jim, ah, Detective Matthews and you were living together for awhile. Then one day he just up and left you. No explanation, no nothing. We heard that you almost suffered another break down, like when your partner was killed. Well, Russ and I don't think that what he did was right. Especially now that we know you and everything, so we decided not to talk to him."

Great, I thought to myself as Bobby explained; now Jim and I are the hot gossip topic in town.

"Guys." I began, "I appreciate the thought but Jim could have arrested you for obstruction of justice. What you did was wrong, no matter what your intentions. Besides, it didn't quite happen that way. We had a fight first, and then he walked out. Promise me that you won't do it again."

"We won't." Bobby and Russ said in unison.

"Okay." I said giving them each a hug. "Now, do either of you know where Matt was working on Saturday?" I asked as I sat back down on the barstool.

"Yeah." Bobby replied, "He was roughing in a house at that new subdivision going up on 26 and River Road."

"Great." I said glancing at my watch. It was almost midnight. "I have to get home. I'll be in touch."

I jumped off my barstool, left some money for the drinks and headed home. I pulled into the garage and went into the house through the laundry room.

I immediately sensed that something was terribly wrong when the dogs didn't greet me. I reached in my bag and pulled out my gun. Without turning on any lights, I cautiously made my way down the hall from the kitchen towards the front door. As I walked, my foot struck something big. I reached down and felt one of the dogs lying on the floor.

Panic overruled my senses and I flipped on the light in the hallway, Rambo was lying at my feet. Sydney was just a few feet away from Rambo, also lying limp and lifeless. I reached down and felt Rambo's chest. He was still breathing, so was Sydney. I could see the steady rise and fall of his chest from where I stood. I blindly ran into the kitchen, grabbed the phone and dialed Jim's number.

"Jim Matthews." He said groggily as he picked up the phone. I could tell he had been asleep by the sound of his voice.

"Jim! Oh God Jim! It's the dogs! I don't know what happened." I gasped into the phone.

"Savannah, calm down. What's wrong?" I could tell he was wide-awake now.

"I don't know. I came home and oh God Jim, he got the dogs." I felt myself becoming hysterical.

"Are the dogs breathing Savannah?" He asked soothingly.

"Yes." I replied, a little calmer, as I walked over to Sydney. "Jim, there's blood on the floor of the foyer."

"Okay," He replied. I could hear the rustling of him getting dressed over the phone. "I'm on the way. I'll get a patrol car there. Just stay calm. Did you check the rest of the house?"

"No. I came in and saw the dogs." I replied, cautiously looking around me as I sat on the floor and stoked Sydney's fur. "I'm going to kill him Jim. I mean it. When I find him, I'm going to kill him."

"Okay." Jim said. "I'm on the way. Get out of the house until the patrol car gets there. Do it Savannah." Jim added firmly.

"Okay." I said meekly as I hung up the phone.

I jumped up from where I was sitting and did a quick search of the rest of the house. All clear, except for the fact that my house looked like a tornado had gone through it.

In the great room the couch and chairs were overturned and the cushions scattered haphazardly around the room. My office was even worse. All my angel statues had been swept off the shelves and were lying shattered on the floor. My file cabinets had been pried open and files scattered everywhere. All the books had been thrown from the shelves on the second floor of the office and were scattered everywhere. My bedroom was in a state of chaos. All of my dresser drawers had been over turned onto the waterbed, and the clothes from my closets were tossed everywhere.

In heard the wail of police sirens in the distance so I went out through the garage and onto the driveway just in time to see Jim's Durango and three squad cars scream to halt in front of my house. Jim leapt from his truck and ran up to me enveloping me in a giant hug. I hugged him back, sobbing hysterically as he held me. Jim broke off the hug and took my gun from my hand and stuck it in the waistband of his jeans. He then led me into the house as the officers gave the all clear.

Jim bent over and carefully examined the dogs. He then walked over to the small amount of blood lying on the foyer floor. The crime scene unit had arrived and Jim borrowed a pair of latex gloves before opening the front door to the house. There were signs of blood on the mail slot on the outside of the front door.

"Let's get the dogs to a vet." Jim said quietly.

Jim and two other officers gently placed the dogs on blankets and carried them out to Jim's truck. He piled me in the truck and we drove down to the emergency vet in town.

After a careful examination the vet withdrew some blood that revealed that the dogs had been fed sleeping pills. The vet said that they would probably be fine, but wanted to keep them for the night to make sure. He would call me tomorrow.

I kissed the dogs good bye and Jim wrapped his arms around me and took me home.

We got back to the house and the crime scene unit was still in the process of gathering evidence. Since they had already processed my office and the basement, I decided to check my safes. I went down to the basement where I had a safe cemented into the wall when the house was being built. It was still locked and all the contents were intact. It appeared as though the intruder had never even gone into the basement.

In my office I have two safes. One is an old bank safe weighing about a thousand pounds. It too had not been opened, although I gave the intruder an "A" for effort. The third safe, located on the second floor of the office behind some fake books was also intact, although the intruder had tried to gain access, but failed.

Jim went into the kitchen and poured me a glass of wine. He then put the cushions back on the couch and chairs and led me to one of the chairs and gave me a blanket. He found my bag by the laundry room door, and after a brief search found my cigarettes and lighter. He retrieved an ashtray from the kitchen and wordlessly handed me a cigarette and lit it for me. I took a deep drag and sat back on the couch. I was numb. After snuffing out my cigarette, I got up and went into the kitchen to get another glass of wine. By the time I got back into the great room I was angry.

"I'm going to find him," I said as I began to pace wildly around the room.

"I know you are Savannah." Jim replied. "We will find him. Now tell me where you were tonight."

I sat back down and told him about the stakeout and following Mrs. Walker to the Fisherman's Bar and Grill. I also told him about talking to Bobby and Ross at the Stop Light Tavern. Just as I finished telling Jim about the events of the evening, one of the crime scene personnel came into the great room.

"Ah, Ms. Williams," the young technician began, "we're all finished here. The lab tests should be in early tomorrow. I put a rush on them. I'm really sorry about your dogs. Are they going to be okay?"

"Yes, thank you," I answered, "They were drugged with sleeping pills. They should be fine."

"Goodnight Ms. Williams, Jim." The technician said and left.

"I'm staying here tonight." Jim said.

"No. I'll be alright." I answered. I just wanted to be alone. My head was pounding and I was exhausted.

"That wasn't a question Savannah," Jim said firmly, "that was a statement of fact. I am not leaving you here alone."

Too weak and tired to argue, I got Jim a pillow and blanket from the linen closet. I walked back into the great room, tossed them on the couch, walked into my bedroom and shut the door. I pushed all the clothes that had been emptied from my dresser drawers to the floor, got undressed and crawled into bed.

As I got into bed I realized that I didn't tell Jim about the car that had followed me and that I thought the man in the car was the same man who broke into my house. I started to get out of bed to tell Jim and then stopped. No. Someone had invaded my private space and that was unacceptable. He was mine.

CHAPTER 8

▼

I woke up to the intoxicating aroma of freshly brewed coffee and allowed myself a long, luxurious stretch before rolling out of bed. I had to dig through the piles of clothes on the floor until I found my robe and padded out of my bedroom into the office to survey the damage. Jim had replaced the books and had swept my broken angels into a pile in the middle of the floor. The files that had been haphazardly strewn about were all stacked neatly into two piles on my desk. One pile held the file folders, the other the contents.

Totally depressed I strolled into the kitchen to get a cup of coffee. I found a note on the kitchen counter from Jim saying that he would call or stop by later. After pouring my coffee I called the vet and found out that the dogs were awake and doing fine and that I could pick them up later that afternoon.

Feeling a little better, I wandered back into my bedroom to take a shower. I had a lot of work to do today. After finishing my shower, I got dressed and headed back into the office to sort out and put away my files and finish cleaning up the pile of broken angels.

I started cleaning up the angels, when I came across the body of a beautiful crystal angel that Frank had given me for my birthday two years ago. It had stood about eight inches high and depicted an angel with long hair and arched wings. It was kneeling with its hands folded in prayer. Frank had said that he bought it because it reminded him of me. Now all that was left was the body, the wings had been broken. I sat down amid the ruins of my den, hugged the angel and began to cry.

After allowing myself a few minutes of self-pity, I regained my composure and began cleaning up the den. I replaced the broken angel on one of the shelves by my desk and began the long process of putting my files back in order.

I took a break around ten and decided to drive out to the job site Matt had been working on the day he was killed.

The job site was located way out in the country and was surrounded by cornfields. Apparently the developer had only bought a portion of the farmer's holdings and there were houses rising out of the ground like overgrown weeds. I drove aimlessly through the new subdivision until I spotted some roughers working feverishly to raise a wall on a new house. I pulled over to the side of the road, got out of my jeep and headed in their direction.

After talking to one of the roughers I was directed to Bill Watkins, the foreman of the crew. I took a few seconds to study Mr. Watkins before I approached him. He was medium height and built like a brick wall. His brown hair was cut short and his skin the color of tanned leather. I walked up to him and introduced myself.

"Hi, Mr. Watkins. My name's Savannah Williams. I'm the profiler working on Matt Winter's murder. May I talk to you a couple of minutes?" I smiled sweetly as I spoke and extended my hand.

Mr. Watkins shook my hand. It was deeply callused from his work. "Sure, and please call me Bill." he responded, "Shame about Matt. I liked him. He was a good worker. What do you want to know?"

Mr. Watkins face was open and honest and his dark brown eyes looked right back into mine. I liked him instantly.

"Were you working the Saturday that Matt disappeared?" I asked.

"Yeah, I was here for awhile. We were working on the house across the street." Bill responded pointing to a huge roughed in colonial. "Matt and I were working on getting up the rest of the interior walls.

We wanted to get the house finished so we could start this one on Monday."

"What time did you leave?" I asked.

"I left the same time Matt did. About noon. He said he had a side job building a deck." Bill said, his handsome face crinkled up in thought," Matt was the one guy I could always depend on you know?"

"Yes I do." I replied solemnly.

"Did Matt say where the deck building job was?" I asked excitedly.

"No. He didn't. Oh God." Bill said, rubbing his hand across his face. "I let Matt go meet his killer."

"Bill," I said softly, putting my hand on his broad, well-muscled shoulder, "there was nothing you could have done."

Bill gently took my hand in his. "Thank you for that. Please, just find out who did this and stop him."

"I will. You can count on it." I said with conviction. My eyes welled up with tears as I remembered Sydney and Rambo's limp bodies lying on the floor last night.

"This is personal for you, isn't it?" Bill asked curiously. "Do you want to tell me why?"

"The killer broke into my house last night while I was out and almost killed my dogs. I forgot to set the alarm." I responded as I tried to choke back the tears.

Bill reached out and wiped away a stray tear that had managed to roll down my face and then gave me in a big hug.

"I'm sorry." Bill said, releasing me from his arms obviously embarrassed by his spontaneity. "Are your dogs going to be okay?"

"Yes. They are going to be fine. In fact," I said looking at my watch, "I have to go pick them up from the vets." I was trying to extract myself from a very awkward situation. Although I have to admit I enjoyed the hug. "Here's my card. Please call me if you think of anything else that might help." I said. Not daring to look into his eyes.

"Thanks." Bill said, carefully putting the card in his wallet.

I turned around and headed back to my jeep.

"Savannah," Bill yelled from across the street, "Can I just call you?"

I turned around and looked at him. "Yeah," I said laughing. "You can just call me."

I got into my jeep and headed to the vets to pick up the dogs. I knew it was early, but I couldn't wait.

I drove to the vets and after paying the bill received an enthusiastic greeting from the dogs. They gleefully jumped into the back of the jeep and we headed home.

Upon arriving home I turned them loose in the backyard and went into the kitchen to check the answering machine. There were two messages. One from Jim saying the lab tests were back and one from Andy asking me to call him.

I picked up the phone and dialed Jim's number.

"Jim Matthews." He answered.

"Hi Jim. What did the lab tests show?" I asked.

"There were no unidentified fingerprints." Jim responded, as he shuffled through some papers on his desk. "The tests showed that the blood on the mail slot and floor is cow's blood. The theory is that whoever broke in fed the dogs meat laced with sleeping pills and then simply waited until the pills took effect. There were signs of forced entry on the doorwall."

"So," I began, "whoever it was has been watching the house long enough to know that I have the dogs and that I normally work at night." I finished thinking about the car that had been parking behind the house and the car that followed me last night. I didn't think it was the same car, but I couldn't be sure.

"I would say so, yes." Jim answered.

"Thanks for picking up the den for me." I said gratefully.

"No problem." Jim said, "Anything new?"

I told him about my conversation with Bill Watkins at the construction site and after a few more minutes talking, we hung up.

I then dialed Andy's number and he answered on the first ring. We made plans to get together later in the afternoon.

I spent a few hours cleaning up the house and at four o'clock the doorbell rang.

"Hey, Andy." I said as I opened the door.

Andy was dressed in a green camouflage T-shirt and jeans. I swear the snake tattoo on his arm moved as he reached out to open the storm door. He was carrying a large briefcase and set it down on the floor as he entered.

Rambo and Sydney gave Andy a raucous greeting and Andy spent a couple of minutes petting and making the appropriate noises over them.

"Hey Savannah, how's it going?" Andy responded, "Nice dogs."

"Thanks. Can I get you something to drink?" I asked.

"A Coke if you have it."

I led Andy into the kitchen and retrieved two Cokes out of the refrigerator and gave one to Andy.

"I thought we would be more comfortable working in my office." I said.

"Great. Let me get my briefcase." Andy headed back to the foyer, picked up his briefcase and followed me into the office. As he entered the office he noticed the garbage bag by the office door. It had fallen open revealing the broken angels.

"What happened?" Andy asked curiously.

I explained to him the events of the past few weeks and the incident last night.

"Curious." Andy said, after listening intently to my dissertation. "What was he looking for?"

"I'm not really sure." I responded. "Nothing seems to be missing, but he couldn't gain access to my safes.

"What's in the safes?" Andy asked.

"Current case files and some case files from when I was with the Bureau." I answered. "Whatever he was looking for I don't think he found. In fact," I continued, "I think it may be more of a scare tactic on his part."

"Possible, but I don't think so." Andy said. "I think he was looking for something very specific. Either something you don't have and he doesn't know it, or something you have and you just don't realize its significance."

"Good point." I answered. "Shall we get started?" I asked as I opened the big safe and extracted my files on the murders.

I gave Andy the files and he spent a few minutes reviewing them. He set aside the pictures of the symbols and carefully replaced the rest of the paperwork back in the files. He then opened his briefcase and extracted two books. After what seemed like forever, but was in reality only a few minutes, Andy looked up at me.

"Got it." Andy said triumphantly. "The symbols at Mr. Maxwell's murder scene are from the Kabalistic alphabet. Some of the letters of the Kabalistic alphabet correspond directly to a specific tarot card. It was created by 19th century occultists in France and England and is often referred to as the "Christian Kabbalah" to keep it separated from purely Jewish Kabalistic line of thought."

When Andy mentioned the tarot cards, I felt a shiver race along my spine like icy fingertips against bare skin.

"The symbols translate to N. O. O. N. E." Andy said, as he finished deciphering the symbols.

"No one?" I asked. "What the hell is that supposed to mean?"

"I don't know," Andy responded, "but what is even more curious is that the only letter in "no one" that directly corresponds to a tarot card is the letter "N". In the tarot it is the death card."

"But the death card does not mean death in the tarot." I said, as I reached for the tarot book on my desk and began thumbing through the pages. "If the card is not reversed it means renewal, transformation. Birth of new ideas. Destruction of the old, followed by the new. If the card is reversed it means temporary stagnation. It could also mean death of a political figure, political upheaval. Disaster." I added, as I read from the book.

"And since we don't know which way the card would be, we have no way of interpreting its meaning." Andy surmised.

"Unless," I conjectured, "the killer was just being literal. "N" equals death which would make the disposition of the card irrelevant."

"That would make more sense." Andy agreed. "What I find even more fascinating is the pentagram."

"What do you mean?" I asked, picking up the picture and studying it for a couple of seconds.

"Well," Andy began, "everybody knows that a pentagram is a five pointed star. However, if the top triangle is pointed up it means life, if the top triangle is pointed down, like the one in the picture, it symbolizes the devil."

"Interesting", I said as I lit a cigarette, "but I don't think the killings were done by a cult or cult member. I think the killer is just using the symbols and pentagram as a tool to convey a message. Granted, the killer is ritualistic but I don't see him involved in cult or satanic rituals. The killings aren't brutal enough."

"Murder is always brutal Savannah," Andy interjected, "but I see your point. The killer went out of his way to make sure the victims didn't suffer. In fact, according to the autopsy reports, the victims were more than likely unconscious at the time of death due to the poison. What does that say?"

"It says," I conjectured, "that the killer is unusual in the fact that for some killers, seeing the victim suffer is what gets them off. This guy isn't like that. Which makes me think he is killing for somebody's benefit, to get the attention of someone specific.

"He's killing for you." Andy said flatly. "It's the only thing that makes sense based on what you've told me. You were associated with the victims. He knew that if he killed someone you knew, you would get involved. This killer is someone who knows you Savannah. He knows how you think, knows how you work. He made the killings irresistible to you. Hell, he might as well have dumped the bodies in your front yard. Add to that, I'm ninety-nine point nine percent sure he broke in here last night not only to retrieve something but to send you a message."

What message is that? I asked, already knowing the answer.

"He can get to you anytime he wants and there's nothing you can do about it." Andy answered quietly.

"What about the symbols in Matt's murder?" I asked, quickly changing the subject.

"They are from the Runic alphabet." Andy replied, referring to another book. "The Runic alphabet is one of the oldest forms of the Germanic alphabet. They were also used extensively in Nordic countries. They are used for many different things, meditation, healing, fortune telling and magic. The symbols used in Matt's murder spell N. O. T. W. O."

"No Two." I said curiously. "Is there any correlation between the Runic alphabet and the Tarot?"

"None that I know of." Andy replied.

I took a few seconds and wrote the two deciphered messages on a piece of paper.

"Wait a minute." I said excitedly. "He isn't saying no one or no two, he's counting his victims. What he is really saying is number one and number two. He's just using an abbreviation for the word number because there aren't enough spaces in a pentagram to spell it out. Look!"

Andy picked up the picture of a pentagram and the deciphered symbols.

"I think you're right Savannah. So when is he going to stop counting?" Andy asked apprehensively.

I answered quietly. "He won't stop until we stop him. Which at his current pace of killing better be soon."

CHAPTER 9

▼

Andy left a few minutes later and I headed back into my office to call Jim and tell him what I learned.

"So what's new?" I asked after filling Jim in on the results of Andy and my findings.

"The Chief has called a press conference for eight tonight. He wants a statement from you to give to the press. They're circling like blood-hounds, we have to feed them something." Jim responded.

"Tell them that the killer is a white male in his early to mid-thirties, well educated and articulate." I replied, checking my case file.

"That's it? That's all you have?" Jim asked incredulously.

"No, that's not all I have, but that's all I want to give them." I answered. "What else are you releasing?" I asked curiously.

"Not much. Just that we have two victims, both young white males probably killed by the same person." Jim answered. "We have decided to hold back the pentagrams and the symbols written in blood. Although the Chief does want us to mention that both victims received tarot cards in the mail before their deaths."

"That's probably a good idea. If someone receives a card in the mail, we need to know immediately." I said. "The Chief doesn't want me there does he?" I asked tentatively. I hated press conferences.

"No, not that he mentioned to me. I think it's just going to be him, Ben and myself." Jim answered.

"Good." I said breathing a sigh of relief. "Call me when it's over."

After chatting for a few minutes Jim and I hung up. I barely had the phone back in its cradle before it rang again.

"Savannah Williams." I answered.

"Hi Savannah, its Bill Perkins, from the construction site."

"Hi Bill, what's up?" I asked, noticing that my heart was racing at the sound of his voice.

"Listen, I was wondering if you would like to have dinner tonight. I know it's short notice, but I just got off work." Bill asked hopefully.

I glanced at the clock. It was six thirty.

"I'd love to." I answered warmly. "What time?"

"Great. How's seven thirty? I'll pick you up." Bill replied. I could hear the relief in his voice.

"Fine." I said, and after giving Bill directions, hung up.

I fed the dogs and then raced into the bathroom to take a shower and get ready. After my shower I donned a new pair of blue jeans and a delicate pink blouse. I quickly dried my hair and pulled it back in a waist length ponytail and applied a little makeup. I hated wearing makeup, but after all it was a date. The first one since Jim and I had split.

At exactly seven-thirty the doorbell rang. It was Bill with the most beautiful bouquet of Calla lilies I had ever seen. Bill was dressed in a pair of black jeans and a white polo shirt, both of which fit him in all the right places. I'm not sure, but I think I swooned at the sight of him. I turned on some lights, closed all the blinds, put the flowers in a vase of water, set the alarm and we were off.

We drove up the coast of Lake St. Clair and pulled into the Fisher-man's Bar and Grill, the same place I had followed Mrs. Walker to a couple of nights ago. Bill's choice of restaurants was probably a coincidence, but I was as nervous as a cat when we got out of the car. How could I be so stupid? I knew nothing about this guy. Chalking my reaction up to being paranoid, I shoved my nerves aside and became determined to have a good time.

We went into the restaurant and Bill ordered a bottle of wine. White Zinfandel, my favorite.

"How did you know that this is my favorite wine?" I asked casually, taking my first sip of the delicious liquid.

"Lucky guess. You just looked like a white zin kind of woman." Bill answered smiling.

Not good enough I thought. My senses were on high alert and I was cursing myself for not putting my gun in my purse before we left the house.

"A white zin kind of woman?" I asked, trying to keep my voice casual.

"Yeah," Bill replied, "You've got class and style. Somehow, I just couldn't picture you downing a bottle of beer."

"I like beer." I said somewhat defensively. "But wine is my favorite." I added quickly, smoothing out the harsh tone that had entered my voice.

As we looked over the menu, I caught a glimpse of the news conference on the TV over the bar. The camera was showing a close up of Jim and I felt a twinge of guilt as his face filled the screen. The sound was turned down and I couldn't hear what was being said.

Bill, following my line of sight, saw me staring at the television.

"Friend of yours?" Bill asked.

"Primary detective on Matt's murder." I responded absently, trying to read Jim's lips as he spoke.

"Like I said," Bill continued, "friend of yours?"

"Yes, I suppose he's a friend." I answered carefully, not taking my eyes off the screen as the station flashed Jim's name across the bottom of the screen.

"Look at me Savannah." Bill said somewhat sternly.

I broke my gaze away from the TV and faced Bill.

"You two were more than just friends, weren't you?" Bill asked, his eyes probing mine.

"Yes." I answered defeated. There was no point hiding it. "Jim and I lived together up until about a month ago. Whatever we had is over. It ended when he walked out the door."

"It might have ended for him," Bill said quietly, "but I don't think it ended for you. Maybe we should go."

"No." I said defiantly. "I don't want to go. I was really just trying to figure out what was being said. I'm sorry. I didn't mean to become so distracted. It's just that these murders are making me nuts. I have to stop this guy."

Before Bill could respond, the waitress approached our table to take our order. I ordered broiled salmon and a salad. While Bill was ordering I stole a quick glance at the TV. The press conference had ended.

During dinner I made a consorted effort to keep my attention on Bill, but Jim's face kept whirling in the back of my head. He had looked drawn and tired and very stressed out. I couldn't blame him. My nerves were as tight as a drum too.

Bill and I left the restaurant a little after nine. Bill suggested stopping at a bar where they had dancing, but I really just wanted to go home. I was exhausted. When we got a little way down my street I saw a multitude of news vans parked outside my house and reporters mulling around my yard. What was up with that?

"Quick." I said to Bill as I took a dive off the front seat onto the floor of his truck, "Keep going around the block. Don't even slow down just go."

"Why are all the news trucks around your house?" Bill asked in wonderment, as he drove past my house and turned down the side street.

"I don't know." I answered as I extracted myself from the floor of his truck. I had Bill turn off his headlights and directed him to the circle court that ran behind my house and turn off the engine as the truck stopped.

"Listen." I said turning to face him on the seat. "I'm not sure what this is all about, but I don't want you to get caught in the middle of it. I'm going to jump the fence and go in through the side door of the garage. I had a really nice time, and I'm sorry about all this."

"You are not going in there alone. I'm coming with you." Bill answered.

Great, just what I didn't need right now, a guy with a macho attitude. I knew if I argued with him I would be wasting valuable seconds. It wouldn't take long for the reporters to catch on at my attempt to dodge them.

"Fine." I said quietly but with authority as I pulled my house keys out of my bag. "We go out of the truck at the same time and don't slam the door. Just close it enough to turn off the interior lights. Head for the middle of the back yard, jump the fence and stay low. Follow me. On three."

We both slid out of the truck and headed for the fence, staying as low as possible. When we reached the fence we scaled it quickly and quietly, all the while I was thanking the gods for making me order a vinyl fence instead of a metal one. Once over the fence we made our way across the deck and I quietly opened the gate, letting Bill go through ahead of me and closed it without a sound. I noiselessly slid my key in the lock of the side door of the garage and once we were both through, locked it behind us. We entered the house and I locked the door and turned off the alarm. We were home free.

Wordlessly I tossed my bag and keys on the kitchen counter, grabbed the phone and began dialing. The dogs came in to greet us barking furiously, so I gave them rawhide bones to keep them quiet and occupied.

"Jim Matthews." He had answered on the second ring.

"What in the hell is going on?!" I said loudly into the phone, barely giving Jim enough time to say his name.

"Savannah? What in the hell are you talking about?" I could hear the confusion in Jim's voice as he responded.

"What am I talking about?" I said angrily as I poured a large glass of wine. "Why is every TV station in the state camped out in front of my house? What did you say at the news conference?"

"You know what I was going to say." Jim responded. "I didn't do this Savannah. Haven't you been watching the news?"

"No." I said, lowering my tone of voice. "I was on a date. What happened?"

"After the news conference, someone called the stations anonymously and said that you knew both the victims." Jim said. "We are presuming the call came from the killer and are in the process of getting copies of the call, if they were recorded. You're going to have to give them a statement Savannah. Where are you now?"

"In my house. I jumped the back fence and came in through the side door of the garage." I answered, neglecting to tell him that Bill was still here. "I am not going to give them a statement. That is exactly what the killer wants me to do. He wants the attention. Unless.." I said. An idea was beginning to form in my head.

"Unless what, Savannah. I don't like that tone of voice. What are you going to do?" Jim asked suspiciously.

"I'm not quite sure yet, but keep your eyes on your TV screen. I am not going to play his game, but perhaps I can get him to play mine." I said confidently, as the plan began to take shape.

"Don't you do anything until I get there, and that's an order." Jim said sternly. "I know you too well Savannah. Sit tight, I'm on the way." With those words Jim hung up the phone.

I gulped my glass of wine and poured another. Bill and I kept out of sight of the front windows, but I have to admit I did take a peek or two. After about ten minutes I heard a soft tapping on my doorwall. Cautiously I peered out through the blinds and saw Jim and the Chief standing at the door. Apparently they had taken the same route I had to get here. I opened the door and let them in.

After I introduced everybody to Bill, I pulled him aside and took him into the great room.

"Listen Bill." I said turning to face him. "This could get ugly real fast. I need you to go."

"I'm not leaving you with a yard full of reporters." Bill replied.

"Bill, first of all, you can't be seen here. It's for your own protection. I don't want you to be the killer's next victim. Secondly, I'm working now. This is what I do. I'm going to let you out the doorwall. Jump the fence, get in your truck, start driving and keep going. Don't stop until you are home. Don't go to the bar, don't stop for gas, don't stop for anything. Do you understand? Your life may depend on it. This guy isn't fooling around. He's as serious as a heart attack." I said as sternly as possible to get my point across.

Bill, finally realizing the gravity of the situation finally assented. I let him out the doorwall and watched him climb the fence. He got into his truck and left, not turning on his headlights until he was headed away from my house. I locked the doorwall and closed the blinds.

"Okay, Savannah," the Chief began, "what do you have in mind?"

"I think its time I drew the killer out into the open. It's the last thing he is expecting. Would either of you care for something to drink?" I asked nonchalantly, as I took another sip of wine.

"No thank you." They responded tersely and in unison.

"If you think I'm going to let you offer yourself up as bait you've got another thing coming." Jim said vehemently.

"I'm with Jim on this one Savannah. It's too dangerous." The Chief said.

"Don't you guys get it?" I asked, "He's not going to come for me. It's too soon. The game's just started for him. He's not going to let it end, not yet. I just want to throw off his timing. Make him regroup. It's a gamble," I admitted, "but if I don't do something, he's going to kill again, and soon. I feel it. I'm just going to try to buy us some time so we can figure this thing out."

"What if you're wrong?" Jim asked quietly.

"Then I'm wrong. Let him come after me. I'd rather have him come after me than kill another innocent person. At least I will be expecting it and can take steps to protect myself." I answered.

"Does life really hold so little meaning for you that you would sacrifice yourself? Don't you have a reason to live?" Jim asked angrily.

I thought about Frank's lifeless body lying in a pool of blood on his front yard. I thought about Jim's angry and hateful words before he walked out the door a month ago. I turned and looked at the Chief, and at Jim.

"Not anymore." I responded and walked out the front door to meet the reporters before Jim or the Chief could stop me.

The reporters, seeing me emerge from the house, swarmed the porch like bees to honey. Jim and the Chief had no choice but to follow. The Chief and Jim stood stoically on either side of me. I felt like a midget.

"Ladies and Gentlemen. I am going to make a brief statement and will be taking no questions. It has come to my attention that an anonymous caller telephoned all of you within minutes after the news conference held by Chief Briggs, Detective Matthews and Detective Mills informing you that I knew both victims. That information is correct. I was briefly acquainted with both victims. It is also correct that I have been hired as the profiler for these crimes and that a short profile of the perpetrator was provided to you earlier. Now, here's what you weren't told. The perpetrator is killing for my benefit, to get my attention. Well, he's got it. I know he is out there, close by, watching this. So this is for him. You are a coward. You want me? Come and get me. But remember one thing, if I go down, I'm taking you with me. You can count on it."

I turned my back and walked into the house. The Chief and Jim followed. Jim walked into the office and looked out of the front blinds. The reporters were beginning to disburse.

"Do you think it worked?" The Chief asked.

"I hope so. I'll know by tomorrow." I responded as I walked into the kitchen and took a big drink of wine.

"What makes you so sure?" Jim asked, joining the Chief and I in the kitchen.

"The killer won't be able to resist responding to what I said. He'll contact me directly, not through the press. I just made this very personal for him." I answered as I lit a cigarette and took a big drag, inhaling deeply. "I just threw his whole game off by confronting him. He needs time to think, time to plan." I said more confidently than I felt. With that statement I walked into my bedroom to retrieve my gun and a full clip. Upon returning to the kitchen I looked at both of them.

"Lock and load gentlemen." I said, slamming the clip home, "Let the game begin." I said firmly.

"Okay," the Chief began. "Now for a little planning on our part. I'm going to call the station and have unmarked cars patrol the house every fifteen minutes. Jim, you go home and pack some clothes. You are going to be staying here until this guy is behind bars. I'll stay with Savannah until you get back."

"No way!" I exclaimed, looking at the Chief like he just developed two heads. "Jim is not staying here."

"Sorry Savannah, but I'm pulling rank here. Jim is staying here and I expect you two to act like you are back together when you are out in public. I'm not going to make it easy for this guy to get to you and I'm not going to make it easy for you to kill yourself. If you want to commit suicide you are going to have to do it on your own time, not on mine. Understood?" The Chief said firmly.

I knew the look on the Chief's face. It was the same look my father used to give me when I had done something stupid. There was no point in arguing.

"Yes sir," I said resigned to the fact that I had lost. I looked over at Jim who was leaning against the kitchen counter with a slight grin on his face, "but he's sleeping on the couch."

"Jim, you better get going." The Chief said, trying to hide the smile that played across his face.

"On my way Sir." Jim said as he walked over to the doorwall. "Be back in a little while honey." He said with mocked sweetness as he let himself out and shut the door, avoiding the glass of wine that I threw at him.

"You really need to do something about that temper of yours Savannah." The Chief said as he grabbed some paper towels and began cleaning up the shattered glass on the floor.

"I can't believe you did that to me. You know Jim and I are barely on speaking terms. We can't be in the same room together for more than five minutes without being at each other's throats. What were you thinking?" I asked sounding more like a small child than a grown woman.

"Listen Savannah." The Chief said as he threw away the soiled paper towels and then turned to me and put one big hand on each of my shoulders, his eyes becoming gentle as he spoke to me, "I know about the breakdown you suffered when Frank was murdered. I know when you and Jim broke up a month ago you almost suffered another one. I know you feel responsible for Mr. Maxwell and Matt's deaths. I also know that you are under a tremendous amount of stress and judging by your actions tonight not thinking logically. You left me no choice. If you won't protect yourself, I have to do it for you."

"So you think I'm irrational and ready to have another breakdown." I said as I shrugged the Chiefs hands off my shoulders and poured another glass of wine.

"No Savannah, I don't think you are irrational, you just didn't think things through logically. I think you did what you felt you had to do. As for having another breakdown, no I don't think you are ready to have another one; you are stronger than I thought. I just want to keep you that way. Okay?" the Chief asked with a pleading look in his eyes.

"Okay." I agreed, like I had a choice.

The Chief used my phone to call the station and arrange for the patrols on my house. Soon after that Jim returned and the Chief left.

"Do you want to sleep on the couch or in the guest room upstairs?" I asked Jim wearily.

"The couch is fine for tonight." Jim responded.

Too tired to ask him what that remark meant, I made up his bed on the couch and let the dogs out.

Sydney and Rambo immediately headed for the back fence and began barking. Jim and I each grabbed our guns and headed out the doorwall after them. Staying in the shadows, we carefully made our way back to the dogs.

"See anything?" Jim whispered from behind the big oak tree next to the fence.

"No." I lied, whispering back. I saw the car that had been watching my house backed into the driveway of a partially finished ranch house on the left side of the court, it was impossible for Jim to see the car from his angle, but clearly visible from mine. I could barely hear the running of the engine over the dog's barking.

"Probably just a deer or raccoon. Let's go back in." I said in a normal tone of voice.

Jim and I headed back to the house and called in the dogs. I gave them each a treat and headed into my bedroom. I got changed into my nightgown and put my gun under my pillow. I heard Jim check all the doors and set the alarm before turning out the lights. I quietly opened my bedroom window and heard the car pull out of the driveway; I saw his taillights as he pulled out of the court. I shut the window, locked it and got into bed followed closely by Sydney and Rambo.

I was slept soundly until two a. m. and that's when all hell broke loose.

CHAPTER 10

▼

The first bullet crashed through the window in my office. Total chaos followed. The alarm sounded on impact. The dogs leapt off the bed and began barking furiously at the bedroom door. I rolled out of bed grabbing for my gun from underneath the pillow as I hit the floor. I crawled into the master bath, coaxing the dogs to follow. I put them in the shower stall and shut the door. I then crawled out of the bathroom towards the bedroom door. Careful not to expose my body to the door, which was in a direct line with the office window, I reached up and opened the bedroom door wide enough to crawl through. The bullets kept flying, I could hear them shattering through the windows and front door and several whizzed over my head and lodged themselves somewhere behind me.

"Jim!" I shrieked my voice high with panic.

There was no response and I was basically trapped. If I continued down the hallway towards the front of the house I had no protection from the bullets that were rocketing themselves through the front door.

"Jim!" I yelled again, realizing that the couch was in direct alignment with the front door. "Where are you? Are you okay?"

Again there was no response.

I crawled back into my bedroom and shut the door. I could hear the dogs barking wildly in the bathroom and was surprised that Rambo hadn't launched himself through the shower door yet.

I reached the phone along side my bed and dialed 911.

"911 Emergency. May I help you?" A calm male voice answered.

"Yes, This is Savannah Williams, there is someone shooting up the front of my house. I can't get out of my bedroom and I'm afraid Detective Matthews has been shot. I need a car out here fast!" I breathed panic stricken into the phone.

"I have cars on the way Ms. Williams. Can you see the perpetrator?" the voice on the phone asked.

"No I can't see the perpetrator." I screamed into the phone. "Would you like me to go open the front door and ask him to wait until you get here?" I asked sarcastically.

"Of course not." The voice responded, "If you would just calm down so that I can get some more information. The cars should be there momentarily."

"The shooting has stopped." I said, a little calmer. "Hold on. Oh, and if it's not too much trouble do you think you could send an ambulance?"

Not waiting for a response, I hung up the phone, jumped off the floor and ran out of my bedroom and into the great room. Jim was lying on the floor by the couch, his gun in his hand. Blood was soaking the front of his shirt and dripping onto the carpet.

I ran to the linen closet, grabbed a couple of towels and applied pressure to the wound.

"Jim!" I screamed. "Don't you dare die on me! I still love you."

"I love you too." Jim answered, opening his eyes, and then shutting them again lapsing back into unconsciousness.

I heard the squad cars screaming down my street and stop in front of the house. I ran to the front door and threw it open. I ran out onto the lawn.

"Hurry," I said hysterically, "Jim, I mean Detective Matthews has been shot. Where's the damn ambulance?"

"It's on the way Ms. Williams. I'm Officer Patrick. Where's Detective Matthews?"

"On the living room floor. It's bad." I responded, leading them into the house.

I ran back over to Jim and kept applying pressure to the wound in his stomach. I felt for a pulse. He was still alive.

The ambulance arrived a few seconds later and the paramedics began working on Jim.

"Ms. Williams," Officer Patrick began, "who or what is locked in your bathroom?"

"The dogs. I forgot about the dogs." I said, running in the bathroom to release them from their make shift prison. They came bounding out of the bathroom and into the great room. They were both nervous wrecks. Sydney began pacing from room to room and Rambo stalked around the house stiff legged and growling at everybody and everything.

"Ms. Williams," Officer Patrick said nervously, easing his way towards the front door to avoid Rambo's clenched jowls and throaty growl. "Perhaps it would be better if you locked the dogs back up until we have concluded our investigation."

I called the dogs and shut them in the bedroom giving them each a treat. I rushed back out to talk to the paramedics who were working feverishly on Jim.

"How bad is it?" I asked tensely.

"It's bad." One of the paramedics responded. "We are going to transport him to Macomb Hospital immediately."

I watched as the paramedics carefully laid Jim on the stretcher and rolled him out to the ambulance.

I raced by the officers and evidence technicians swarming over my house and ran back into my bedroom to get dressed. My nightgown and hands were soaked in Jim's blood and I choked back tears as I washed my hands and threw on a pair of jeans and a T-shirt. I tossed my gun in my purse and headed through the house towards the garage.

"Where are going?" Officer Patrick asked, stopping me as I got to the kitchen.

"To the hospital to be with Jim." I responded as I tried to sidestep him to get to the door.

"We need you here. You have to make a statement." Officer Patrick stated.

"I'll make a statement tomorrow. Lock up when you're finished and let the dogs out of my bedroom before you go." I answered and then continued, "If the alarm company decides to call to see if everything's alright, tell them no it's not and thanks for their concern." I added as I neatly moved around Officer Patrick and headed out into the garage.

My hands were shaking so terribly I could barely get the key in the ignition and start my jeep. I started to back out of my driveway when I discovered that police cars blocked the end of the driveway. Not having any other choice, I jerked the jeep into four wheel drive and drove over the lawn to the street, taking out a couple of the hedges that line my driveway as I went. Oh well, I hated them anyway.

I made it to the hospital quickly and after parking my jeep, raced into the emergency entrance to find Jim.

I spoke with one of the emergency nurses who directed me up to the fifth floor where Jim was undergoing emergency surgery. They weren't giving odds as to his chances of survival.

I pressed the button for the elevator and ran my hands through my hair in frustration. What was taking the elevator so long? Giving up, I raced down the hallway and found the stairs. Taking them two at a time, I reached the fifth floor in record time and totally out of breath. I made a mental note to give up smoking; once this case was over.

I checked in with the duty nurse and sat down in the surgical waiting area to wait for the doctor. It was then that the horror of the whole situation caught up with me and I began to sob uncontrollably.

I regained my composure just in time to see the Chief roll through the door of the waiting room. He spotted me and headed in my direction. Without a word, one of his big, beefy hands reached out, grabbed my arm and led me out of the waiting room and into the hallway.

"Damn it Savannah. What in hell were you thinking?" He asked me gruffly.

"What in the hell are you talking about?" I asked, shocked at his tone of voice.

"I'm talking about the fact that I received a frantic phone call from Officer Patrick about you leaving him at your house without giving a statement and your damn dogs locked in the bedroom ready to tear anybody's head off that comes near them. You know better than to leave a crime scene" The Chief finished.

"I'm sorry" I began, "but I needed to get here to be with Jim. If Officer Patrick can't handle processing a crime scene and two dogs without someone there to hold his hand it's not my problem. Do you have his number? I'll call him."

I called Officer Patrick and told him where the rawhide bones were kept so he could give one to each of the dogs. I explained that it would calm them down and he would become their best friend. I waited on the line while he retrieved the rawhide bones and fed them to the dogs that gratefully took the treats and contentedly settled in on the floor of the kitchen to eat. After hanging up I turned my attention back to the Chief.

God, I'm sorry Savannah," the Chief began, "I was so angry with you I didn't ask about Jim. How is he?"

"It's not good." I responded, my eyes welling up with tears. "He's in surgery. They don't know whether he's going to make it."

I totally broke down as I finished and the Chief enveloped me in a bear hug until I calmed down.

"How's Jim?" A concerned voice asked as I pulled myself out of the Chief's arms.

I turned around to see Ben standing next to the Chief. The Chief explained everything to Ben and we returned to the waiting room and sat down. Ben got the Chief and I a cup of coffee than sat down with his arm around me in silence until the surgeon approached us.

"Detective Matthews is out of surgery." He began. "He is in recovery and will be transferred to intensive care. He got lucky. The bullet just nicked his heart, but we were able to repair the damage. He should be fine in a few weeks. You will be able to see him tomorrow. Any questions?"

All three of us stood and breathed a collective sigh of relief. We had no questions, so I said good-bye to the Chief and Ben and headed home. The police had left, but Sandra's car was in my driveway. It was seven a.m. I was exhausted.

"Land sakes alive," Sandra said as I walked into the house. "What the hell happened?"

I quickly explained the situation to Sandra who sat and stared at me in shocked disbelief. Leaving Sandra in the kitchen, I walked into the foyer to survey the damage. Cone shaped bullet holes had riddled my front door and the brick on the porch. My office walls looked like Swiss cheese. Bullets had lodged themselves in the drywall and the police had practically torn down the wall trying to retrieve them leaving pieces of drywall scattered over my desk and floor. My bedroom door was basically nonexistent and a big pool of blood lay in a puddle next to the couch.

"Jim's going to be fine though, right?" Sandra asked with tears in her eyes as I walked back into the kitchen.

"Yes, he's going to be fine, Sandra." I answered as calmly as possible. "Now, help me clean this place up."

Sandra and I spent the next two hours cleaning up the blood and the drywall. By the time we were finished, my insurance company was open so I called them to report the damage. They promised to have a board-up company come out and board up the office windows with an adjuster to follow later this afternoon, but they weren't happy. Sandra had thoughtfully put on a fresh pot of coffee so I wandered into the kitchen to get some.

"I think you should stay with me for awhile." Sandra said quietly.

"No, Sandra!" I responded rather harshly. "I brought this on myself by antagonizing the killer at the news conference yesterday. I started the game; I have to finish it."

"Savannah," Sandra retorted, equally as harsh, "this is not a game. My God, Jim almost died tonight. This guy means business. You and the dogs are staying with me. End of discussion."

"I am not staying with you Sandra. I am staying here. Some lunatic with a high-powered rifle will not force me out of my own house. I've been running all my life. I'm tired of running. So just resign yourself to the fact that I'm staying. This is my fight and I'm going to fight it my way. If you don't like it you can leave." I regretted my last words the second they came out of my mouth and saw the hurt expression on Sandra's face.

Without a word Sandra rose from her chair at the kitchen table and headed for the front door.

"Sandra, I'm sorry." I said sincerely, stopping her at the foyer. "I didn't mean what I said. I'm just frustrated and upset. I didn't mean to take it out on you."

"I know you didn't, Honey," Sandra said, giving me a big hug. "But now I think you've got a bigger problem."

Sandra motioned towards the front door. I peeked out one of the bullet holes and saw the media vans begin to pull up outside and reporters and cameramen setting up on my front lawn and driveway.

"What are you going to do?" Sandra asked curiously.

"I don't have a clue." I responded. "Do you think if I let them sit out there long enough they'll get bored and leave?"

"Not a chance." We both answered at the same time, laughing.

I walked away from the front door and called the Chief. After a few minutes of discussion, we hung up and I walked back to the front door.

"What did the Chief say?" Sandra asked.

"He told me to punt." I responded.

"What the hell did he mean by that?" Sandra asked.

"I'm not sure." I answered, and with a deep breath opened the front door. "Here goes nothing." I said as I walked out onto the porch.

"Ladies and Gentlemen. As I'm sure you are all aware, Detective Jim Matthews was injured during a drive by shooting that occurred earlier this morning. Detective Matthews underwent emergency surgery and is expected to make a full recovery. The origin of the shooting is still under investigation. There will be another press conference at nine o'clock tomorrow morning at the police station. I have no further comment at this time." With those words I turned and walked back into the house.

"Good job." Sandra said. "I just hope that's what the Chief meant by punting."

"I do too." I responded as Sandra and I watched out of the bullet holes in the front door as the press began to disburse.

"Listen, Savannah," Sandra said turning away from the door, "why don't you get some sleep and I'll stay and watch out for the board-up company and the adjuster."

"Okay, "I answered gratefully," but wake me up by one o'clock. I have to go to the police station and work on the case. I have to come up with something."

"Gotcha." Sandra responded.

I walked into my bedroom and without even bothering to get undressed crawled into bed and fell immediately to sleep.

I was forced out of bed at noon by the sound of someone hammering outside my house. The board-up company must be here. I took a shower and wandered out into the kitchen to find Sandra. Ben was standing at the kitchen counter doling out Chinese food from cardboard cartons.

"Where's Sandra?" I asked, biting into an egg roll.

"She had some errands to run." Ben replied, as he brought the steaming plates of food over to the kitchen table. "I offered to stay here and wait for the board-up company and adjuster. The adjuster was by a little while ago and took a look at the place. He said he would call you the first of the week."

"Oh. Any word on Jim?" I asked hopefully.

"Yeah, I called the hospital when I got here and they said he is resting comfortably and we can see him tomorrow." Ben answered, and then continued, "By the way, the Chief is pretty upset about the press conference stunts you've been pulling the last two days."

"I know, but I don't feel that I had any choice." I responded. "Listen, do me a favor. The board-up company looks like they are about done here, can you call the police station and arrange for the task force assigned to the case to meet me in the conference room at three thirty. It's time we put this thing to bed."

"Sure thing. You got something?" Ben asked curiously.

"Maybe." I answered as I put the plate with the rest of my Chinese food on the floor for the dogs. "But I need some things checked out first."

"Ok." Ben said as he took the empty plates into the kitchen and put them in the dishwasher. "I'm going up to the station to assemble the task force. See you at three thirty."

"I'll be there." I said rising from the table to show Ben out.

"Hang in there." Ben said, giving me a quick hug and kiss on the forehead as he walked out the door.

I signed for the board-up and headed into my office. Time to go to work.

CHAPTER 11

―――――――― ▼ ――――――――

I pulled the case files out of my safe and sat down at my desk. I carefully reread the case file on Mr. Maxwell's murder and made several notes. I then turned my attention to the crime scene photographs. Using my magnifying glass, I went over every inch of the photographs stopping at one of the autopsy photos. The photo depicted Mr. Maxwell lying prone on the table, his arms at his side and a sheet discreetly laid across his torso. Barely noticeable were slight marks around his wrists.

I then turned my attention to the photographs of Matt's autopsy. The same marks were there, but faint. I wondered what could have caused them. They didn't look like rope or wire marks, but somehow they seemed vaguely familiar. After making a few more notes, I placed the files in my briefcase.

I put Sydney and Rambo on their leashes, tucked my gun into the waistband of my jeans and headed out into the woods. I wanted to take another look at where Matt's body had been found.

The dogs and I entered the woods and I let them off their leashes to romp around and chase the squirrels.

I walked over to the tree where Matt's body had been found. Taking a deep breath, I allowed my body to relax and put myself in mind of the killer. It was obvious that Matt was already dead when he was brought to the crime scene. The same theory held true with Mr. Maxwell, or did it?

I knelt down and examined the tree trunk. There were faint indentations where the rope had been tightly tied to the tree. Mr. Maxwell's body had not been tied to anything.

Matt's body had been carefully wrapped in a tarp. Mr. Maxwell's had not. Why? I thought back to the autopsy reports. Mr. Maxwell had been dead only for a few hours and was placed in a garbage dumpster in a concrete parking lot. Matt had been killed Saturday afternoon or early evening and placed in the woods. The tarp was probably to keep animals from getting to Matt's body. The killer didn't want the body to be damaged in any way, other than the tarot card that was meant to convey a message. Plus, I had been late taking the dogs for their walk that day. I was supposed to find Matt earlier.

In Matt's case the killer must have relied on planning and luck. No, the killer planned everything too carefully he was too organized. He would never rely on luck. He must have killed the deer before killing Matt and bringing him here. I headed to the spot where the deer had been found. Yellow police tape was still wrapped securely around the area and I had to duck underneath it to gain access to the site and carefully scanned the ground for any sign of blood from the deer. There was none readily apparent, so I slowly walked the area stopping occasionally to examine the leaves and ground for any sign of dried blood. I didn't see any, but made a mental note to ask the members of the task force if they had found any at the scene and how much.

I glanced at my watch. It was two thirty. After taking the dogs home and giving them fresh water and food, I grabbed my briefcase and headed back out.

I drove up to K Mart and got out to walk the scene where Mr. Maxwell had been found. I wasn't expecting to find anything, but was hoping to get a fresh perspective on his murder. The one thing that struck me as odd was the fact that Mr. Maxwell's car was at the scene. The police still hadn't been able to locate Matt's truck. Not unusual given the miles of country roads in the area. It could be just about anywhere.

Did Matt drive his car to the scene, or had the killer used his car to transport Mr. Maxwell's dead body to the scene? I couldn't imagine Mr. Maxwell meeting someone that late at night in the parking lot of K Mart, so the latter probably held true, unless Mr. Maxwell had known his killer. Possible, after all, Matt and Mr. Maxwell knew each other. Was there a possible connection there?

I got back into my jeep and headed to the police station. As usual, I had more questions then answers.

Upon entering the police station, I stopped and asked one of the secretaries to make some copies for me and then headed into the conference room.

Ben had rounded up all the usual suspects. Cal was there, along with Marge Dawson, the evidence technician working the case. Marge and I had worked on other cases before and knew her work to be impeccable. Her auburn red hair was shoulder length and pulled back into a ponytail. She caught my eye as I entered the room and flashed me quick smile.

Ben was running around the room getting everybody something to drink and making sure that they had their case files with them.

Also present was Detective Brent Marshall, who was relatively new to the force. Station gossip was that he held master's degrees in criminal justice and computer science and was a real brain. He looked the part. His six foot five frame towered above everybody else in the room and he was as skinny as a rail. His thick, black-framed glasses were askew on his face and his bright green eyes were darting nervously around the room. He was even wearing a pocket protector with pens, pencils and a slide ruler. This was obviously the first big case he had been involved in. Ben introduced us and he shook my hand enthusiastically. I couldn't help but smile. He reminded me of an overeager beagle puppy. This was going to be fun and I had a feeling Detective Brent Marshall was going to be quite a big help.

Rounding out the group was Detective Mark Bower. If ever a man was born to be a cop it was Mark Bower. He was considered a cop's cop on the force and went strictly by the book. That could be a problem. I never read the book. He was on loan to the task force from the vice squad. When he walked across the room to get a cup of coffee I couldn't help but notice that for being such a large man, he moved like a cat. His brown hair was cut military style and he was built like a brick wall, tough as nails and all business.

After a few more minutes of chitchat I got everybody to sit down and be quiet so that I could begin the meeting. The secretary that I had given the materials to had discreetly slipped into the room and carefully placed the copies in front of me, originals on top. Good secretary.

"Ladies and Gentlemen," I began, "as you are aware, Detective Matthews was injured in a drive by shooting early this morning. He is expected to be fine. It's up to us to put this thing to bed so lets get started. I'm going to be handing out assignments and I expect some results by seven thirty tomorrow morning."

I turned my attention first to Cal.

"Cal, I need two things from you. I need the time of death for the deer found at the scene of Matt Winter's murder. I also need to know what the ligature marks are on the wrists of both victims." As I spoke, I distributed copies of the photographs of the wrists of both victims.

Cal shuffled through his file. "The deer was killed between nine and ten on Saturday morning. I'll get to work on those marks on the wrist. I made a few notes on them. They appeared at the time to be from some type of bracelets. Unfortunately, both bodies have been released to the families and buried."

"Get them exhumed if you have to." I stated simply. "Get a court order if necessary. I feel that Mrs. Winters will cooperate, but Mrs. Maxwell might be a problem. Work on it."

"You got it." Cal responded making a few notes on the legal pad in front of him.

"Speaking of the deer, "I said turning my attention to Marge, "was there any blood found with the deer at the scene?"

"Yes, quite a lot actually." Marge responded, checking her case file. "Most of it was mixed with the leaves and ground cover. We bagged and tested it. It was definitely deer's blood. The deer might have been shot elsewhere, but it was definitely gutted and drained of blood at the scene."

"Good job." I said warmly, flashing her a big smile. "What else do you have for me?"

"Not much," Marge said despondently, "this guy's real careful. No fingerprints and very little trace evidence. We did find a little bit of skin under Matt's fingernails. We have enough for a DNA analysis and were able to rule out the skin being that of the victim. There were a few specks of lint on Matt Winter's body, but it matched the sheet. There was nothing foreign."

"Okay." I said with a sigh, "Try again. Go over everything one more time, just to make sure."

"I'll get right on it." Marge said, somewhat deflated.

I then distributed the picture of Kenny.

"I need you to find this guy." I said to the group. "All I have is a first name of Kenny. He might be working a construction site. He claims to be a rougher. This man was seen with Mrs. Maxwell a few nights before Mr. Maxwell was killed. I want him in for questioning. He has been avoiding me like the plague."

Detective Bower picked up the photograph and studied it carefully.

"I'll get more copies made and have it distributed to every police officer in the area." He said. "What else do you need me to do?" Detective Bower asked enthusiastically.

"I need you to find Matt Winter's truck. It couldn't have just disappeared off the face of the earth." I answered, as I referred to one of the papers in my file. "Matt Winters drove a nineteen ninety black Dodge pick-up. I made copies of the registration. Distribute it with the photograph of Kenny."

"Not a problem. If it's out there, I'll find it for you." Detective Bower said, relieved that he could get out on the street and not stuck behind a desk.

"What do you want me to do Ms. Williams?" Detective Marshall asked.

"First of all I want you to call me Savannah." I said with a smile. "Secondly, I have a very special assignment for you Detective Marshall. I understand that you have a master's degree in computer science. Is that correct?" I asked.

"Yes Ma'am. I mean Savannah." Detective Marshall said blushing.

"I need you to come over to my house and trace a few e-mails for me. Here is my card with my address on it. I will expect you right after this meeting." I said.

"I can do that Savannah, but isn't that kind of illegal?" Detective Marshall asked.

"God bless your honesty Detective," I answered, "but quite frankly I don't care if it's legal or not. This might be the only way to find the killer."

Detective Marshall nodded his head in assent.

"Ben, you've heard the assignments. Anything you wish to add?" I asked.

"No. I think you've covered all the bases. I'm going to go back out to the construction sites where Matt Winters and Mr. Maxwell were working and talk to their co-workers again. Maybe we missed something."

"Good idea." I responded. "Also, please check to see if the news stations have located the recordings of the killer when he called them to let them know that I am directly connected to the victims. Now, if nobody has anything else. Let's get to work. I expect everybody to meet me back in this room tomorrow morning at seven thirty."

The meeting disbursed and I headed home with Detective Marshall tagging along behind me.

We arrived at the house and I let the dogs out the doorwall. Detective Marshall headed out behind them and a rowdy game of soccer soon ensued. While they were out playing, I decided to fire up my computer and check my e-mail. I had no idea how long he would need to trace the messages from the killer.

I had numerous messages from various police departments requesting help or information. As I scanned the addresses in my inbox, I recognized one as being the killer's. Taking a deep breath I clicked on the message to open it.

Savannah,

I admire your courage. However the game will be played my way. It would be wise to heed the meaning of the Five of Swords in the book I sent you. Upside down or right side up this card holds your fate.

I let out a small scream as I pushed myself away from the computer. I heard Detective Marshall and the dogs race into the house and head for the office.

"Are you okay Savannah?" Detective Marshall asked excitedly as he rushed into the room.

"I'm fine. The killer sent me another message. It just startled me." I said, a little calmer, showing the message to Detective Marshall.

"Wow, this guy is serious. Are you ready for me to get started?" Detective Marshall asked quietly.

"By all means." I said rising from my chair. I let Detective Marshall sit down at the computer and watched in amazement as his fingers flew over the keyboard. My computer was doing things I didn't even know it could do.

Shaking my head in awe, I grabbed the Tarot card book and curled up in one of the overstuffed chairs in the corner of the office.

The Five of Swords right side up means conquest over others by physical strength, or could mean a threat to the person receiving the card. Upside down, the meaning was weakness, chance of loss and defeat. Stormy weather ahead.

The killer was right. Either way I lose.

CHAPTER 12

▼

Afternoon soon turned in early evening as Detective Marshall worked to trace the e-mail account. I spent the afternoon typing up Mr. Walker's report on my laptop, making out his bill and preparing it for mailing.

By five o'clock I was starving and decided to order pizza. When the pizza arrived Detective Marshall and I took a break to eat and discuss his findings.

"I'm getting real close Savannah." Ben said as he munched on another piece of pizza. "Another hour and I should have it nailed down."

"Excellent." I responded as I reached for piece of pizza. "Let's just hope it doesn't lead to another dead end."

"Amen to that." Detective Marshall said, rising from the table and taking his plate to the sink. He then headed back into the office and got down to work.

After about twenty minutes he rose from his chair and stretched.

"This guy's better than I thought. "He said yawning. "I'm going to have to go to my apartment and get some software. I'll be back in about an hour if that's okay"

"Do what you have to do Detective." I responded. "I'll be here.

Detective Marshall left and I went into the kitchen to pour a glass of wine. I had just finished pouring and was taking my first delicious sip when the doorbell rang.

I opened the door to find my friend Rita standing there, obviously distraught. Her five foot seven frame was visibly shaking and her blue eyes were red and puffy from crying. Her shoulder length black hair was mussed, and her face was pale and drawn, giving her an eerie appearance.

"Rita! What on earth is wrong? Come in." I said putting my arm around her and ushering her into the house. I led her into the great room and deposited her on the sofa. I then went into the kitchen and got my wine and poured her a big snifter of brandy. I hurried back into the great room and after giving Rita her brandy, joined her on the couch.

"Oh Savannah." Rita began, "It's terrible. I don't know what to do."

"Shhh. It will be okay. Tell me what's wrong." I said with concern.

"I just left Madame Phoebe's store. I had another reading. Oh Savannah, you've got to stop this investigation now. You have to leave. Get out of town. Please Savannah, I'm begging you." Rita exclaimed, tears welling up in her eyes as she spoke.

"What are you talking about? What did Madame Phoebe say?" I asked.

Rita took a couple of minutes to compose herself and after a big sip of brandy continued.

"Madame Phoebe said that she thought that someone close to me was going to be killed. It was in the cards Savannah. I saw the news about the drive by shooting and Jim getting shot. It has to be you Savannah. If you don't stop this investigation you're going to be killed." Rita said with conviction.

"Rita. I'm not going to be killed." I said with more confidence then I felt. "Besides, you know that Tarot card stuff isn't real, and even if it is, it is all subject to interpretation. I'm going to be fine. Anyway, I'm in too deep to stop now and with Jim being out of commission I don't have any other choice."

"Yes you do." Rita said pleadingly. "Let Ben handle it. He's Jim's partner. He should be the one running the investigation, not you."

"Rita. Ben is a very good detective. But I was hired to be the profiler on this case. The killer is murdering for my benefit. People are dying because of me. I have to stop it. I'm the only one who can. If I disappear God only knows what the killer would do. He could spin totally out of control and a lot more people could end up dying. No Rita. I'm sorry, but I have to finish this. Please try to understand." I said firmly.

"I know you're right Savannah." Rita said, taking another sip of brandy. Please just promise me you'll be careful and not take any unnecessary risks."

"I promise." I said solemnly, holding up two fingers. "Scouts honor."

"You were never a Scout." Rita said laughing.

"I know, but I always wanted to be." I responded laughing with her.

Rita and I chatted a few more minutes and made plans to have lunch sometime next week. I made a mental note to go have a little talk with Madame Phoebe.

Soon after she left Detective Marshall returned and began working on the computer.

A little while later I heard a big whoop come from the office. I raced in to see what he had found.

"I got it Savannah, but you're not going to like it." Detective Marshall said pensively.

"What won't I like?" I asked curiously.

"The killer was quite clever. He routed the messages through a lot of different systems, making me think that I was onto something. But as it turns out, he sent the e-mails from different libraries in the area." Ben said sadly.

"Okay. So all we have to do is get the security tapes from the libraries and scan through them to the times the e-mails were sent. No problem." I responded.

"Not necessarily." Ben answered. "The little libraries he used don't even have security cameras. He probably scoped out the different libraries and only used the ones without surveillance equipment."

"That figures." I responded. "It sounded too easy. I'm sorry I made you waste so much time."

"It wasn't a total waste of time. It just eliminated one avenue of investigation." Detective Marshall responded kindly. "What else do you need me to do?"

"Go back through the case file and re-interview everybody. Maybe they remembered something they didn't tell us before. Also keep an eye open for Matt's truck and Kenny." I answered.

"You got it." Detective Marshall said. "I'll review the file tonight and start interviewing people first thing in the morning."

"Sounds good." I said. "Goodnight Detective."

I let Detective Matthews out and locked the door behind him.

Feeling restless I decided to go up to the hospital and see Jim.

When I got to the hospital I had to show my I.D. to the cop stationed at Jim's door before I was allowed entry into his room.

As I walked into Jim's room I was immediately struck by the silence that hung over the room like a black veil.

Jim was lying in bed deathly still. There were tubes and wires everywhere. I quietly pulled up a chair to Jim's bedside and sat down. I took his hand and began to gently caress it.

I put my head down on the edge of his bed and began to sob quietly.

"Shh. I'll be okay Savannah." A weak voice said from the head of the bed.

"Jim?" I asked incredulously as I raised my head to look at him.

"Hi Honey." Jim responded with a weak smile.

"Hi." I said smiling. "I was so scared. I thought you were dead."

"So did I." Jim said squeezing my hand.

"I'm so sorry Jim. I never should have taunted the killer like that. I never dreamed he would react so harshly. It's all my fault." I said, the words tumbling from my mouth as tears ran down my cheeks.

"It's okay Savannah. It wasn't your fault." Jim said gently. "I don't think he meant to hit anybody. I think it was just his way of responding to the press conference."

"You really think so?" I ask doubtfully.

"Sure. Think about it for a minute." Jim said, warming up to his theory. "You hold a press conference and challenge him in a big way. He has to respond. My truck was in the garage. He has no way of knowing I'm even there. He's been inside your house. If he wanted to kill you he would have shot into your bedroom, or find another way to get to you. He was just saying message received."

"Sounds logical." I responded, still not quite convinced.

"How is the investigation going?" Jim asked curiously.

I filled Jim in on the task force meeting and the results of the e-mail trace.

"Sounds like you have got things under control." Jim said admiringly, and then asked, "What are you going to say at the press conference in the morning?"

"I think I'm going to turn the heat up on Kenny." I responded.

"You really think that's our man?" Jim asked.

"I'm not sure, but I want to have a serious discussion with him." I responded.

As we talked, I could see that Jim was wearing out fast.

"Listen," I said, "I have a lot of work to do before morning. Why don't you get some rest and I'll see you tomorrow okay"

"Okay." Jim said weakly.

I rose from my chair and kissed him on the cheek. I grabbed my purse and headed for the door.

"Savannah." Jim said.

I turned around to face him.

"I meant what I said. I do still love you." Jim said with a slight smile. He must be feeling better if he has the strength to throw me off balance like that.

"Me too." I answered and then blew him a kiss and darted from the room. I swear I heard him chuckle as the door closed behind me.

I got home and took the dogs out in the back yard. The moon was full and there must have been a billion stars lighting up the night sky. While the dogs were busy investigating what creatures were roaming around the perimeter of the yard, I went into the kitchen to pour a glass of wine and retrieve my cigarettes. I rejoined them on the deck and sat down in a deck chair to think about the case. I had to be missing something.

There was a high probability that the killer had purchased the tarot card book that was sent to me at Madame Phoebe's store. Madame Phoebe said that she had sold one of the books to a man. I walked into the house and retrieved the book out of my office. I then picked up the same tarot card book that I had purchased from Madame Phoebe's. I inspected them both carefully and discovered that the book I had bought at Madame Phoebe's had a stamp inside the front cover bearing the name of the store and the address and phone number. The book the killer had sent me had no such stamp or any other information that could identify where the book had been purchased. Upon closer inspection however, I discovered that a page had been carefully cut out from the front of the book.

I sat and continued to roll the case over and over in my head, looking at it from different angles, playing the game of "what if". Coming up empty, I gave up and called the dogs into the house. After making a few notes about the news conference in the morning I went to bed. It had been a bad day and tomorrow didn't look much better.

CHAPTER 13

The sound of the phone ringing brought me out of a luscious dream where I was on a date with Mr. Right. Oh well, I thought as I rolled over to look at the clock, he would probably turn out to be Mr. Wrong just like the rest of them.

I grabbed the phone and looked at the clock. It was five a.m.

"Talk to me." I said as I clicked on the phone.

"Detective Mark Bower calling Ms. Williams." The deep, sexy male voice said into the phone.

I quickly snapped myself out of the risqué thoughts racing through my head at the sound of his voice and tried to focus on the conversation.

"What is it Detective Bower." I asked yawning.

"Sorry to wake you up Ms. Williams, but I found Mr. Winter's vehicle. I called to get your instructions." Detective Bower said.

My eyes flew open and I sat straight up startling the dogs. They jumped off the bed and began barking furiously.

"Call the station and have them get a team out there. I'm on the way." I said.

"Yes Ma'am." Detective Bower responded then paused.

"Oh, by the way, Detective, exactly where is there?" I asked sheepishly.

"Off Twenty-Five Mile Road by Ridge Road. The truck is back in the woods a little bit. Hope you aren't afraid of snakes. I took the liberty of calling for a marked unit. I will have the officer wait by the road and direct you to the site." He responded, all business.

"Good thinking Detective. I'll be there in fifteen minutes." I hung up the phone not even waiting for his response.

I jumped out of bed and took a quick shower. I then wrestled myself into a pair of jeans and knee-high leather boots. I hated snakes. I tossed on a lightweight gray sweatshirt, kissed the dogs good-by and headed out.

I called Sandra on the way to the site and asked her to head out to the house and take care of the dogs. I could tell it was going to be a long day.

Upon arriving at the scene I leapt from my jeep and was directed back into the woods by the officer Detective Bower had waiting for me.

There was a short piece of dirt road that led back into the woods. Detective Bower met me at the end of the road and handed me a strong flashlight. We proceeded past a few small trees and into a clearing surrounded by deeper forest and contained a small pond. Matt's truck was in the center of the pond. Good thing I had worn boots.

"How did you ever find the truck back here?" I asked Detective Bower as we were walking toward the pond.

"It really wasn't all that hard, just time consuming." He responded, "I started looking at the point Mr. Winter's body was found. I figured the perpetrator wouldn't take the truck very far; there was too great a risk of being spotted. I simply fanned out and drove around the area eliminating populated areas and open fields. I came across this little road and saw tire tracks in the dirt that would be the same type as those found on Mr. Winter's vehicle. I walked back here and saw it."

I stood and stared at him in amazement.

"When did you start this search?" I asked curiously.

"About four thirty yesterday afternoon. I stopped around midnight and took a catnap then resumed at approximately four thirty this morning. There was a lot of ground to cover. Sorry it took so long." Detective Bower responded.

"No, no," I said, hiding a smile, "that was a great piece of detective work. Good job."

"Thank you Ms. Williams." Detective Bower said, rather embarrassed by the praise.

Detective Bower and I carefully circled the area around the pond shining the flashlights on the ground in front of us looking for possible footprints or clues. The ground around the pond was soft, so it was quite possible to find something. We didn't get very far before one of the Crime Scene Investigation teams showed up and took over processing the scene. After carefully scanning the scene and marking out footprints and other possible trace evidence, they set up huge halogen lights that lit up the woods. There was nothing we could do except watch and wait. Detective Bower excused himself at one point and returned a little while later with two steaming Styrofoam cups filled with hot chocolate and whipped cream.

"I hope you like hot chocolate." Detective Bower said, handing me the cup.

"It's one of my favorite things." I answered, giving him a warm smile. "Where did you get this?"

"At the gas station a few blocks from here. Is it okay?" He asked with concern.

"Perfect." I said taking another delicious sip. I hadn't had hot chocolate in years and had forgotten how much I liked it.

Detective Bower and I spent some time watching the crime scene personnel work the scene and talking. I finished my hot chocolate and glanced at my watch. It was seven o'clock.

"Oh my God," I exclaimed, "Look at the time. I have to get to the station. There's a press conference in an hour."

"Do you want me to stay here and supervise the removal of the truck to the impound yard?" Detective Bower asked.

"Yes. I'll head to the station and meet with the rest of the team." I answered. "I owe you a steak dinner for this one Detective."

"You don't owe me anything Ms. Williams." Detective Bower responded professionally. "I was just doing my job."

I gave Detective Bower my best smile and walked out of the woods to my jeep. I made it to the station in five minutes flat and hurried inside to meet with the team.

Ben, Marge and Cal joined me in the conference room a few minutes later.

"Morning Savannah." They said in unison as they entered the conference room.

"Hi." I answered. "Let's get busy, we have a lot of ground to cover before the press conference. Has anybody seen Detective Marshall this morning?" I asked, glancing at my watch. It was seven thirty.

The words were barely out of my mouth before the desk sergeant poked his nose into the conference room.

"Ms. Williams, there's a call for you on line two. It's Detective Marshall."

"Hello." I said as I put the phone to my ear.

"Ms. Williams. This is Detective Marshall." He breathed excitedly into the phone.

"Good morning Detective. Where are you?" I asked impatiently.

"I'm at a small apartment complex out on Palms Road. I found Kenny." Detective Marshall said quietly.

"Good work Detective. Bring him in for questioning."

"We'll be there in a few minutes." Detective Marshall responded.

"Okay Detective," I began, "start at the beginning and tell me how you found him."

"Well, last night after I left your place I took Kenny's picture and showed it around the local bars. I started in Ashley and worked my way up to Algonac. I handed out my cards and put my cell phone number on them and told people to call me day or night if they saw Kenny." Detective Marshall began.

"Go ahead." I said, listening intently.

"After I got out of the shower this morning, my girlfriend said that someone had called on my cell phone. Thinking it might be important she answered it. The person on the phone gave her this address. Nothing else. The caller didn't identify himself or herself and unfortunately I don't have caller I.D. I got dressed and drove out here. I banged on the door and no one answered. I tried the doorknob and the door was unlocked so I let myself in. I caught him just coming out of his bedroom. The rest you know." Detective Marshall finished.

"Did your girlfriend say if the caller was a man or woman?" I asked, already knowing the answer.

"A man." Detective Marshall responded. "Hey, wait, you don't think it was the killer who called do you?"

"It could have been." I answered grimly. "Get him in here Detective. I have a lot of questions for that man."

"On the way." Detective Marshall said and then hung up the phone.

I turned my attention to Cal and Marge.

"Cal, did you turn up anything new on those marks around the victim's wrists?" I asked.

"Not yet." Cal responded, "but I'm working on it."

"Good. Since I'm going to be busy for a while, why don't you go back to the morgue. I'm sure you have things to do there." I said.

"You bet." Cal responded and after carefully gathering his materials left the room.

"I know, I know." Marge said smiling. "You want me to go out and help process Mr. Winter's truck. I'm on the way."

"Report to me as soon as you have anything." I responded laughing. "Also," I added, withdrawing the tarot card book the killer had sent me from my briefcase, "I want you to see if you can identify what type of instrument cut one of the pages from this book."

Marge took the book and I showed her where the page had been removed.

"No problem." Marge responded. "I'll get on it when I am finished processing Matt's truck."

"Great. Thanks Marge." I answered with a smile.

"Do you want me to sit in on the interview?" Ben asked.

"That would probably be best." I answered. "I don't want to scare this guy, so no good cop bad cop stuff. Let's just play it straight. Okay?"

"Sure thing." Ben answered.

I looked at my watch. Five minutes to eight. Might as well go feed the wolves.

I left the conference room and walked out the front door of the police station to meet the press.

"Ladies and Gentlemen." I began. "Matt Winter's truck was found early this morning and we are in the process of gathering evidence at the scene. Detective Matthews is doing very well and is expected to be released from the hospital soon. A possible suspect who shall be named at a later date is being brought in for questioning as we speak. I regret that I don't have more to give you at this time, but as you can tell the investigation is moving forward at a rapid pace. I want the public to be aware that this killer does not strike without warning. If anyone receives a tarot card in the mail, they are to contact the police immediately. I'm sorry I can't take any questions at this time. Thank you."

I turned and walked back into the police station leaving a barrage of questions in my wake.

I was met by Detective Marshall who informed me that he had brought Kenny in the back way. Two uniformed officers were in the conference room with Kenny waiting for me.

"Did you read him his rights Detective?" I asked.

"Yes Ms. Williams. He declined counsel." Detective Marshall responded.

I sent Detective Marshall out to re-interview everybody connected with the case and headed into the conference room pausing only to get a tape recorder and fresh tapes.

Kenny sat forlornly at the conference room table. His hands clasped together and lying on the table in front of him. I dismissed the officers and sat down across from Kenny. Ben took his place at the head of the table. I placed the tape recorder on the table and then looked him right in the eye.

"Kenny," I began, "did the Detective that brought you in read you your rights?"

"Yes" Kenny answered.

"Did you understand your rights?" I asked.

"Yes."

"Do you want an attorney present while I talk to you today?" I asked.

"No! I don't need an attorney I have nothing to hide. I didn't do anything wrong." Kenny responded, leaping out of the chair.

Ben got up and put his hands on Kenny's shoulders.

"Sit down!" Ben commanded.

Kenny sat back down.

"Okay," I said, "Let's get started. Do you have any identification on you?"

"Yes." He said and pulled out a worn black leather wallet from his back pocket. He carefully extracted his driver's license and slid it across the table towards me.

I picked it up and studied it for a few minutes. His real name was Kenneth Blackstone. He was thirty years old. Funny, I thought he was older. I excused myself for a minute and handed the license to one of the officers stationed outside the door.

"Please run this guy through every database we have." I said firmly.

"Yes Ma'am." The officer responded and headed off to find a computer. I sent the other officer for coffee from the donut place down the street.

I sat back down and turned my attention back to Kenny.

"Tell me Mr. Blackstone," I began, careful to keep my voice non-threatening, "where were you the night Mr. Maxwell was murdered?"

"I was at my apartment." Kenny said noncommittally.

"Mr. Blackstone." I said. "We know you were having an affair with Tabitha Maxwell. Now, tell me the truth. "Where were you the night Mr. Maxwell was murdered?" I asked again.

"I was at my apartment with Tabby." Kenny said deflated. "I had just leased the apartment that day. Tabby and I had spent the day buying some furniture from Goodwill and had stopped by the grocery store. I guess we got to the apartment about four thirty. Tabby left and went home and I spent the rest of the afternoon putting stuff away. Tabby came back over around 10:30 and was all upset because her and Robby had a fight. She left around 11:00 and I went to bed around eleven thirty after the news."

"What time did you wake up?" I asked.

"The alarm went off at five thirty. I had to be at work by six thirty." Kenny responded.

"Where do you work?" I asked.

"At the new construction site at Twenty-Six Mile and County Line. I'm a finish carpenter." Kenny responded.

"I thought you were a rougher?" I said, baiting him.

"I can do both." Kenny answered.

The officer I had sent out for coffee returned and quietly slipped into the room setting the coffees down on the table along with a stack of cream and sugar and plastic coffee stirrers. I gave a cup to Kenny and he methodically dumped three sugars and three creams into his coffee. He picked up a coffee stirrer and mixed everything up before replacing the stirrer on the table. He then took a long sip of coffee. Ben and I each prepared our coffee and then I started in on Kenny again.

"Back to Tabitha Maxwell for a minute," I began, "Wasn't Mrs. Maxwell afraid that her husband would come home and not find her there?"

"Not really." Kenny said, and then continued. "Robbie knew about the affair and their marriage was basically over. Tabby told me that Robbie had moved into the spare bedroom until he could find an apartment."

"I see," I said quietly. "What else did Tabby tell you?"

"She told me that Robbie had gotten some kind of weird card in the mail and had accused her of sending it. Other than that, she really didn't say anything else. Just that she was mad at Robbie for hiring you to follow us because she was going to try to let Robbie down easy. You know what I mean?" Kenny asked.

"Yes," I responded, "I know what you mean. Now, do you want to tell me why both of you freaked out when you saw me at the gun and knife show at the flea market?"

"Tabby was afraid of you. She thought that you blamed her for Robbie's murder. She thought you were there to arrest her." Kenny answered.

"Why would she think that?" I asked curiously.

"She said that you were pretty hard on her when you came by the house and that you thought she killed Robbie." Kenny explained.

I thumbed through my file on Robbie Maxwell's death and pulled out the tarot card that he received in the mail. I slid it across the table towards Kenny.

"Mr. Blackstone. Do you recognize this?" I asked, carefully watching his response.

His eyes showed no sign of recognition or fear as he studied the card. He then slid it back across the table towards me.

"No, what is it?" He asked.

"It's a tarot card." I responded. "In fact, it's the tarot card Robbie Maxwell received in the mail a couple of days before he died."

"That must be the weird card Tabby mentioned." Kenny responded.

"Now, Mr. Blackstone, have you ever been to Mr. & Mrs. Maxwell's house?" I asked, knowing the answer.

"Yeah, I've been there." Kenny said.

"How many times?" I asked. This was like pulling teeth. I hated interrogations.

"Five or six." Kenny responded.

"Five or six times before Mr. Maxwell was killed, after Mr. Maxwell was killed or all together?" I asked.

"Before he was killed. Since he was killed I haven't been over there as much."

"When you were over there before Mr. Maxwell as killed, did you ever see this card or others similar?" I asked.

"No. I've never seen cards like that in my life." Kenny answered.

"Are you and Tabitha Maxwell still seeing each other?" I asked curiously.

"Yeah, but not very much since the cops are watching her house." Kenny responded.

"What does the fact that the cops are watching the house have to do with anything?" I said.

"Tabitha thinks that if we see each other a lot until the murder is solved that you will think we did it. But we didn't." Kenny answered with an annoying whine to his voice.

I hate whiners.

This was getting me nowhere fast, so I decided to change tactics.

"Mr. Blackstone. Do you own any guns?"

"No. I was going to buy a hunting rifle but changed my mind. I decided to stick to bow and arrow hunting. It's more of a challenge." Kenny answered with a gleam in his eye.

"I'm sure it is." I said. "Did you know Matt Winters?"

"Who?" Kenny asked.

"Matt Winters, the second victim." I said.

"I saw his picture in the paper and he looked familiar but I couldn't place him." Kenny said with a thoughtful look on his face.

"You talked to him about a job after Mr. Maxwell was murdered. It was at the construction site on Sass just south of Twenty-Four Mile Road. Ring a bell?" I asked with a slight edge to my voice.

Kenny thought for a moment and then said, "Yeah, that's where I saw him. He told me to go to the construction trailer and talk to the foreman. Some guy named Bill Perkins."

"Did you talk to Mr. Perkins about a job Kenny?" I asked.

"Yeah, he said he had all the help he needed but to check back in a couple of weeks. Then I got the job I have now and never went back there." Kenny answered.

I excused myself from the conference room and went out to see if the computer had turned up anything on Kenny Blackstone. The officer told me that he was wanted on possession of marijuana in Mt. Clemens. Other than that, Kenny Blackstone was clean. No arrests, no record. The Mt. Clemens Police Department had been called and they were sending a car over to pick him up. Bond was two hundred dollars.

Armed with this information, I returned to the conference room.

"Mr. Blackstone, were you aware that there is an outstanding warrant out of Mt. Clements for possession of marijuana?" I asked.

"Yeah, I knew about it, but jeez, it was just marijuana and that was from a year ago." Kenny said in that annoying whiny voice.

"Nonetheless, you will be transferred to Mt. Clements on that charge. Your bond is $200.00. If you make bond and are released, it would be in your own best interest not to leave town. I might want to talk to you again. Understood?" I said in a firm voice.

"I understand. I won't leave town. Can I say something off the record?" Kenny asked.

I reached out and turned off the tape recorder.

"Go ahead." I responded.

"Tabby and I had nothing to do with Robbie getting killed. In fact, Tabby was real broken up about it. In her own way, she loved him. It just didn't work out between them. As for that other guy, Matt, I only talked to him once and I know Tabby doesn't know him. I really hope you find the guy that's doing this. Maybe then Tabby and I can get on with our lives. Understand?" Kenny said pleadingly.

I understand, Mr. Blackstone. But let me say this again. Don't leave town." I responded.

There was a soft tap at the door and two Mt. Clements policemen came in, handcuffed Kenny and led him from the room.

"What do you think?" Ben asked.

"I think we struck out." I responded. "What about you?"

"I tend to agree, but I'm going to get a warrant to search his apartment." Ben said.

"Let me know if you come up with anything interesting." I said.

"You got it." Ben answered with a wink.

I picked up the phone and called for an evidence technician to come to the conference room. I wanted the cup Mr. Blackstone drank his coffee from processed for prints and possible DNA evidence.

Once the technician left the room, I looked at Ben.

"Ben, I think maybe you should go have another talk with Mrs. Maxwell. Maybe she will respond better to you than she did to me. I have a feeling she knows a lot more than she's saying." I said thoughtfully.

"I'll give it a shot." Ben responded giving me a wink. "What are you going to do today?"

"I have to go to Madame Phoebe's shop. Rita stopped by yesterday and was quite upset by something Madame Phoebe told her. I'm going to have a polite but firm talk with Madame Phoebe about scaring the wits out of her clients and for good measure I'll throw something in about ethical responsibility." I responded with a slight laugh. "After that, I'm going home to work on the case"

"Sounds like a plan. I'll stop by later. I'm going to get that warrant, go talk to Mrs. Maxwell and stop by the hospital to see Jim." Ben said.

"He'll like that. I saw him for a few minutes last night." I said with a smile.

"How is he?" Ben asked.

"He's weak. So don't stay too long and overtax him." I said with a concerned note in my voice.

Ben rose from the table and walked over and kissed me on the forehead.

"Don't worry Savannah. I'll stick to sports and the weather." Ben said, and then left.

I rewound the tape in the recorder and put it in my briefcase. I looked at the clock; eleven thirty. I gathered my things and headed out the door totally dejected. I could have sworn Kenny was our guy. I stopped and asked the desk sergeant to run a search for any vehicles owed by Kenny and he typed the information into the computer. In a matter of a few minutes the computer gave me a printout of all vehicles registered to Kenny. Without looking at it, I jammed it in my briefcase and headed out the front door. I made it to my jeep just before a vicious clap of thunder and streak of lightening roared across the sky. Sheets of rain pummeled the ground as I slowly drove into Mt. Clemens to pay Madame Phoebe a visit. On the way, I telephoned my house and Sandra informed me that the dogs were fine and that the thunderstorm had knocked out the power. I told her I would be home in a couple of hours and to wait for me. I would stop and get Chinese food and we would camp out in the great room. She readily agreed which was no great surprise Sandra loves Chinese food more than apple turnovers and donuts.

I had just hung up with Sandra when my cell phone rang. Thinking it was Sandra telling me what to order, I clicked on the phone.

"What do you want from the restaurant?" I asked, waiting for her laundry list of favorites. Instead I heard the mechanically altered voice of the killer.

"It would be in your own best interest to back off." The eerie voice said over the phone.

"Why is that? What's wrong? Am I getting too close?" I asked in a firm voice. I could not let this guy get to me.

The only response was the click of him hanging up the phone. Maybe Kenny was our guy after all.

CHAPTER 14

▼

I glanced at the clock on the dashboard of my jeep. It had been an hour since Kenny had been taken to the police department in Mt. Clements. I grabbed my cell phone and dialed the number for the Mt. Clements police department. The desk sergeant informed me that Kenny had paid his bond and had been released about fifteen minutes ago.

Storing away that little bit of information, I found a place to park near Madame Phoebe's shop and headed in to talk with Madame Phoebe. Madame Phoebe's cat proceeded to wind itself around my legs while emitting an awesome purr. To keep from tripping I reached down and picked it up and cuddled it in my arms while looking for Madame Phoebe.

I heard Madame Phoebe talking to someone in the back of the store so I headed that way and unceremoniously deposited the cat on one of the overstuffed chairs. I bided my time until Madame Phoebe had finished with her customer and we were alone in the shop.

"Madame Phoebe," I began, "may I talk to you a few minutes?"

"Of course." Madame Phoebe answered looking up at me. I could see the recognition in her eyes.

"I'm here about my friend, Rita. You gave her a reading yesterday that had her quite upset." I said.

"I only tell what the cards show." Madame Phoebe responded, than continued, "You are Savannah Williams aren't you?"

"Yes." I answered. "Why do you want to know?"

"I have seen your press conferences. You are in a bad situation." Madame Phoebe said gravely.

"Nothing I can't handle." I replied rather defensively.

"I'm sure you will handle it quite well, but at what cost?" Madame Phoebe asked.

"The price is always high when it comes to murder. You just have to be ready to pay it." I answered.

"Maybe I can help you." Madame Phoebe said with confidence. "Tell me, what cards has the killer given you to play with?"

"Mostly cards of the sword." I replied tentatively.

"Ah. That would make sense." Madame Phoebe said in a matter of fact tone of voice.

"Why?" I asked curiously.

"The cards of the sword represent force, aggression, misfortune. They are cards of action both constructive and in your case, destructive."

"Hmm," I said thoughtfully, "What can you tell me about the wand cards?"

"Wand cards suggest growth, glory. They too can be constructive or destructive. Your killer is definitely sending you a message." Madame Phoebe responded.

"Yes he is. Now I just have to figure out who he is from the messages." I responded ruefully.

"Not an easy task I'm afraid." Madame Phoebe said pensively. "The cards themselves while being a clue to his identity are not going to lead you to him. You need to look deeper."

"Deeper how?" I asked.

"Do you have some time? "Madame Phoebe asked.

"A little, why?" I said.

"I'm going to close up the shop for awhile and make some tea. I would like you to join me. Maybe I can help you. We should talk." Madame Phoebe said as she put the closed sign on the door and locked it.

I followed her through a curtain at the back of the shop and into a small room with a coffee maker, two chairs and a small table draped with a cheerful red tablecloth. She motioned me into a chair and began making some tea. Without a word, she pulled out an ashtray and placed it on the table. Once the tea was finished she placed the steaming cups on the table and sat down. She lit up a cigarette, took a long sip of tea and turned to me.

I hate tea, but not wanting to be rude, took a sip. It was delicious. I lit up a cigarette and looked at Madame Phoebe.

"This is great tea. What kind is it?" I asked.

"A special blend. I thought you would like it." Madame Phoebe said pleased. "Now tell me what you know about the killer so far."

No having much of a choice. I told her about the tarot cards and the symbols left in the pentagram at the scene and what the symbols meant. Madame Phoebe sat sipping her tea and listening intently. After I finished, Madame Phoebe took a few minutes to digest all that I had told her. Finally, after about five minutes she spoke.

"As I'm sure you have already surmised. These are not the first killings this man has committed. He is too good; too practiced. You need to look into your past. You will find him there." Madame Phoebe said confidently.

"That's what you meant by looking deeper." I said, then suddenly had a brief flash of brilliance, something that doesn't happen very often. "Madame Phoebe, you have been a great help. Thank you." I said as I jumped from the table and headed out into the store. I unlocked the front door and raced to my jeep. I had work to do.

It was still raining hard and it took me what seemed like forever to get home. The power was still out in the area and my garage door opener wouldn't work so I was forced to park my jeep in the driveway next to Sandra's black BMW and make a run for the front door.

I had just made it in the house when I remembered that I was supposed to pick up Chinese food.

"Hi Sandra. Thanks for coming over to take care of the dogs. I forgot the Chinese food. Do you want to run and get it I have a few phone calls to make?" I said breathlessly as I came through the door.

Sandra had lit candles all over the house that cast an eerie glow throughout the rooms. She was curled up in one of my overstuffed chairs reading a magazine.

"Sure, I'll go." Sandra said. "You look like a woman on a mission."

"I am." I responded firmly.

Sandra got her car keys and purse and headed out the front door. "Be back in a few." She said cheerfully as the door closed behind her.

I raced into my office, lit a few candles and grabbed my phone book. I rapidly flipped through my phone book until I found Clint Mayfield's number. Clint worked in the FBI as a profiler and was a good friend. I dialed his number and he answered in two rings.

"Clint Mayfield. May I help you?" His strong, deep southern voice said into the phone.

"Hi Clint. It's Savannah Williams." I said into the phone.

"Savannah! How the hell are you?" Clint responded enthusiastically.

"Fine Clint. How are things there?" I asked.

"Not the same since you left darlin." He responded with his deep Texas drawl. "What's up?"

"Listen. I need a favor." I said expectantly.

"Anything, just name it." Clint responded.

I spent the next few minutes outlining the case. I had to pause every minute or two so Clint could take notes.

"So basically what you need is for me to run this guy's modus operandi through the computer and see what it spits out right?" Clint asked.

"Exactly." I said relieved.

"How soon do you need it? "Clint asked.

"Yesterday." I responded with a laugh.

"Just like old times. You always needed things yesterday." Clint said laughing back. "I'll get right on it. Give me your numbers, I'll call you when I have something."

I gave Clint my home number, cell number and fax number. For good measure I even threw in my e-mail address.

"Thanks Clint. I owe you one." I said gratefully.

"You don't owe me a thing darlin." Clint responded. "Just promise me you'll be careful. Call me if you need help and I'll jump on the next plane out there."

"I will. Talk to you later." I said ringing off, satisfied with the results of my call.

Sandra had come back and was dishing up Chinese food when I got off the phone.

"Sorry it took so long," Sandra said, "the line at the restaurant was terrible."

"No problem. I just finished up anyway." I said biting into an egg roll.

"So," Sandra said, her emerald eyes flashing, "Are you going to tell me what you're up to?"

"Nope." I answered wickedly.

"That's not fair Savannah!" Sandra said shocked.

"Okay. Let's make a deal, if it pans out I'll tell you. If it doesn't I won't." I replied with fake seriousness.

"Deal." Sandra said begrudgingly. "Shake on it."

Sandra and I solemnly shook hands.

We spent the rest of the day chatting and playing with the dogs. Sydney and Rambo get real nervous during thunderstorms so we tried to keep them occupied. The adjuster called about the damage done to the house from the drive by shooting and said that work could begin anytime.

"Great." I said to Sandra as I hung up the phone with the adjuster, now I just need to find a reliable contractor.

"What about that Billy guy you had the date with the other night. Isn't he a carpenter?" Sandra asked with a slight smile.

"Yes Bill is a carpenter, and stop your matchmaking. I know that smile. But, it might be an idea." I responded laughing.

I dug Bill's number out of my purse and called his cell phone.

"Bill Perkins." Bill answered on the third ring.

"Hi Bill. It's Savannah. Listen would you be interested in a little bit of carpentry work on the side?" I asked sweetly. I looked over at Sandra who was looking at me with a self-satisfied smile on her face. I stuck my tongue out at her and she started to laugh.

"Yeah." Bill responded. "For who?"

"Me." I said and explained about the shooting.

After Bill got over his initial shock and I was forced to listen to a fifteen-minute dissertation about the dangers of my job, Bill finally calmed down and said,

"Listen, I'm off today because of the rain, why don't I come over to take a look at the damage and see what materials you need."

"Sounds great, but the power is out, you probably won't be able to see much." I responded.

"No problem. I've got a couple of generators you can use. They won't run the whole house, but at least you can use a few lights and your computer if you have to. I'll be over in about an hour." Bill said gallantly.

"The generators would be great. Thanks a lot." I said gratefully.

Bill and I hung up and Sandra got up to leave.

"I'm going to head home. I've got a lot of work to do." Sandra said.

"Big project?" I asked. Sandra had her own advertisement firm and was quite successful.

"Yes. I have a huge presentation due in a few days and I haven't even started the layout yet. Call if you need anything." Sandra replied and let herself out the door.

I went back into the office and called the electric company. The power was expected to be out at least twenty-four hours. With a heavy sigh, I headed into the great room to wait for Bill.

Bill arrived a short time later and after hooking up one of the generators in the kitchen and the other generator in my office I was able to turn on a few lights, my refrigerator, coffee maker and computer.

Bill spent a great deal of time measuring and inspecting the damage. After doing some figuring we agreed on a price. Bill left to go to the local home improvement store to pick up some of the supplies and get started repairing some of the drywall and replacing my bedroom and front doors tonight. I also asked him to pick up some dinner.

Bill got back around six thirty and after we devoured some burgers and fries, he got started replacing the front door. The door was too heavy to wield by himself so he called his brother who came over to help.

By nine thirty the front door and my bedroom door had been replaced. Bill's brother left and Bill said that he would be over tomorrow to start on the drywall. He had ordered the new windows for my office when he was at the store and they would be delivered in about two weeks.

After thanking Bill profusely, I made him leave and wandered into the kitchen to pour a glass of wine and do some work on the computer.

Ben had called about seven thirty and I gave him an update on what Madame Phoebe had told me and that I was waiting for information from the FBI. I called Jim, who Ben told me had been moved out of intensive care and into a regular room. After chatting with Jim for a while, I flipped on my computer to check my e-mail. There were the usual e-mails and then I spotted one from an address I knew was one the killer had used before. Taking a deep breath and a big gulp of wine for courage, I opened it.

CHAPTER 15

▼

The e-mail read:

> *Savannah,*
>
> *You have been a bad girl. The press conferences have got to stop. You will be punished!*

"Punished!" I screamed out loud as I got up and began to pace the room. "What the hell does he mean by punished?" I stormed around the house checking the windows and doors. I let the dogs out and when they came back in I set the alarm thanking God I had spent the extra money and ordered the battery back up for the alarm system.

Feeling restless, I poured another glass of wine and went back into the office taking my gun with me. I needed to think. Why was the killer so upset about the press conferences? Was I getting close? Was the Kenny the killer? How and when was I going to be "punished" as the killer put it? Too many questions and not enough answers.

I called Ben and asked him to call the other members of the task force and have them assembled in the conference room by eight o'clock in the morning. I knew tomorrow was Sunday, but murder waits for no one. Even God. I told Ben to make sure that the lab would have the test results from Matt's truck ready and waiting for me when I walked in the station in the morning.

By the time I got off the phone with Ben it was almost eleven o'clock. I spent a couple more hours making notes on the case and then went to bed. I had a feeling I was in for another long day.

Sometime around two a.m. the dogs started barking furiously. I grabbed my gun and rolled out of bed. It took a couple of seconds for me to realize that the power had come back on and that the dogs were barking at the television that was blaring in the great room. I wandered out of my bedroom and shut off the TV and the lights that had been on before the power was out and turned off the generators. I got the dogs calmed down, reset all the clocks and then went back to bed. I spent the night tossing and turning. The events of the case were rolling through my head like thunder. I hate that there is no off switch for your brain when you're trying to sleep.

Finally about five thirty a.m., I abandoned all thoughts of sleep and got out of bed and took a hot shower. I got dressed and went into the kitchen to make coffee. The dogs, that had slept blissfully the remainder of the night and were full of energy, scampered after me. I let them outside and they gleefully raced around the yard in a playful game of tag. They stayed out until a loud clap of thunder chased them onto the deck and I let them in the house. They were soaked.

"I just love the smell of wet dogs." I told them as I retrieved two old towels from the laundry room cabinet and began drying them off. This was a total exercise in futility, as they grabbed the towels and a rowdy game of tug of war ensued. There is no winning a game of tug of war with a Golden Retriever and a Rottweiler. They dragged me around the house until I surrendered in a heap on the floor of my office. I ended the game by leaping from the floor and announcing it was breakfast time.

The only thing the dogs liked more than playing was eating. They followed me into the kitchen and I fed them each one huge scoop of dog food and a can of dog food as a treat. They devoured their food in seconds flat making those happy little eating noises only dogs can get away with.

While the dogs were eating, I went into my office to gather my files for this morning's meeting. I glanced at the clock in my office. It was only six thirty.

With time to kill before I had to be at the station, I took out my case notes and went back over them. I knew there was something there that I had missed, but I just couldn't see it. By seven thirty the pieces of the puzzle were beginning to fall into place. The only problem was I was missing one crucial piece; one I was hoping Clint and the FBI computer would be able to give me.

Before packing up my briefcase I decided that since it was still raining, I would give the auto start a try on the jeep. I hadn't played with it yet. I walked out onto the front porch and hit the auto start button on my key fob.

An earsplitting explosion ripped through the morning air as my jeep erupted into a ball of fire. The second I heard the noise I hit the floor of the porch and covered my head as pieces of my jeep rained down around me. When it had stopped I got up and looked at the mere shell of what was once my jeep. Flames were shooting out the windows and the tires were melting and quickly becoming a part of the cement driveway. The hedges along both sides of the driveway were engulfed in flames. Okay, so there was an up side to all this. I hated those hedges. My neighbors came rushing from their houses to see what the noise was. They gathered around the end of my driveway and just stood looking at me with their mouths agape. Not wanting to make a big deal about the whole situation, I smiled meekly and said, "Oops, wrong button."

I quickly turned tail and went back into the house to call the fire department. I didn't want the flames from the jeep and the hedges reaching the house.

The fire department was there in less than five minutes and quickly had the fire extinguished. The police were not far behind. Boy did I have a lot of explaining to do.

To my surprise, Detective Bower pulled up in his truck and came running into the house.

"Are you okay Savannah?" He asked, his voice full of concern.

"I'm fine. What are you doing here?" I responded.

"I heard the call on my police radio. I raced over here to see what had happened." Detective Bower replied. "Are you sure you're okay?"

"I'm just fine, but the same can't be said about my jeep." I responded sadly.

"Do you need me to do anything?" Detective Bower asked.

Obviously being a man of action, he felt helpless unless given a task.

"Yes. Call the station and have them send Marge and the rest of the crime scene unit out here. I need to know if the jeep blew up because of a faulty part or if it was a bomb and I need to know now. Then have the rest of the team assemble here instead of the station. Oh, and have Marge or somebody grab the lab results from Matt's truck and bring them here." I said barking out orders in a stiletto fashion.

"Done. Just show me to a phone." Detective Bower responded relieved at having something to do.

I led him into my office and he attacked the phone like a bulldog. I wandered back outside to survey the damage. The fire department was just finishing up and was getting ready to leave. I thanked them profusely before they pulled away in their trucks.

The neighbors were still mulling around talking amongst themselves and I gave them a friendly wave and a cheerful good morning before walking back into the house.

Detective Bower was waiting for me when I came back inside.

"The crime scene unit and the rest of the team are on the way over. I'm going to go outside and make sure that the uniformed officers secure the scene properly. At least it has stopped raining"

"Thank you." I said gratefully. "The neighbors have had about enough of me anyway."

"It's been pretty active around your place lately." Detective Bower said with a wink as he walked out the front door. Having nothing else to do at the moment, I followed him.

Just when I thought things couldn't get any worse, Bill showed up to work on the drywall with an army of television crews in tow.

"What did I do to deserve this?" I asked looking up at the sky.

Detective Bower, quickly summing up the situation and seeing the look of desperation on my face moved to head off the television crews.

"People, there is nothing here to see. Please leave" Detective Bower said with an authoritative tone to his deep bass voice.

"What happened?" One of the reporters asked, holding out a microphone.

"Just a little accident with Ms. William's jeep. Everyone's fine. There is nothing here. Please leave before I have you removed." Detective Bower answered losing his patience.

"On what grounds?" Another reporter asked angrily.

"On the grounds that you are interfering a police investigation. Now scat! If and when Ms. Williams decides to make a statement you will be notified." Detective Bower said firmly.

Realizing that they were defeated, the television crews began to pack up their equipment and leave.

I wish I could say the same for Bill. Bill got out of his truck that he parked by the curb and with a look of total bewilderment on his face, slowly circled the charred frame of my jeep.

"Savannah, what the hell happened?" Bill asked as he finally made his way up to the porch where I was standing.

"You heard Detective Bower, just a little accident with my jeep." I replied as nonchalantly as possible.

"Just a little accident!?" Bill exclaimed. "The damn thing was blown sky high!"

"Not really." I responded professionally. "By most standards it was really quite a small, contained explosion."

Bill ran his hands through his hair in exasperation.

"That's it. That's enough." Bill screamed, his face becoming red. "You could have been killed! You are quitting this case right now! No woman of mine is going to put herself in this kind of danger. First you're house is shot up, than your jeep is blown to bits. You're done! You're finished. End of story."

I had to hand it to Bill. He knew all the buttons to push; unfortunately they were the wrong ones.

"Just back up the bus Mister." I screamed back. "First of all I am not "your woman" as you put it. Second of all I am not quitting this case. No one, I mean no one tells me what to. Got it?"

Before Bill could respond, Ben came flying up onto the porch and got in between Bill and I.

"If I were you," Ben said sternly, "I would get back into your truck and leave. Now. You have no right to attack Savannah like that. Don't you think she has been through enough for one day?"

"You're right." Bill said calming down. "I was just so scared something had happened to her. I'm sorry Savannah."

"That's okay. Let's just forget it." I responded with about as much graciousness as I could muster. "Why don't you go in the house and get started on the drywall. I have a lot of work to do."

Wordlessly Bill walked into the house and began to move the furniture out of the way in the office so that he could replace the drywall.

By this time the rest of the task force had shown up with the exception of Cal.

Marge got her team busy trying to find out what had caused my jeep to explode and then joined Ben and I on the porch.

We all filed into the house and after getting coffee, settled in the great room to get to work.

"Where's Cal?" I asked casually.

"There's a big accident on the freeway." Detective Bower answered. "There was a fatality so Cal had to go process the body. He said he'd catch up with you later."

"Are you sure you're okay Savannah." Ben asked. "We can do this later."

"No." I responded firmly. "We need to do this now. I'm fine. Marge, let's start with you. Did the lab tests on Matt's truck result in anything?"

"Yes." Marge said, obviously pleased "But first we should discuss your truck. From what I can tell, a small pipe bomb was attached to your gas tank then wired into the ignition switch. I will know more later on today. Now for Matt Winter's truck. We managed to pick up a few fibers, some of which we are still working to identify. We have some denim fibers that don't match the jeans Mr. Winters was wearing when his body was found. I'm going to call Mrs. Winters today and see if I can get some fiber samples from all of the blue jeans Matt owned and see if we have a match. We also found traces of blood. We have been able to identify the blood as having come from the deer. That sample was found in the driver's seat. On the passenger side of the truck we also found some human blood that matches the victim. We found some carpet fibers that we have not been able to identify yet only because of the lack of time. I have the lab techs working overtime though and should have more results in later today. Oh, and that page missing from that book you gave me was removed by a very sharp knife, either an exacto knife or something like it." Marge concluded with a flourish.

"Excellent." I responded cheerfully. "Good work. I have placed a call to an old friend at the FBI. He is running our murders through the FBI computer to see if there are any around the country that are similar. I know this isn't the first time our killer has struck. I hope to have something back from him today. Detective Mitchell, any luck interviewing the witnesses?"

"Not really. Their stories are about the same. I haven't finished with everybody yet so I hope to turn up something." Detective Mitchell said consulting his small black notebook that he kept in his shirt pocket.

"Detective Bower, what about you?" I asked.

"Actually, I did turn up something." Detective Bower said. "Late last night while I was going over some paperwork at the station the printout on Kenny Blackstone's fingerprints came through. Turns out that he has a few different names. Kenny Black, Kenneth Stone, and Kenny Putnam. Mr. Blackstone, or whatever his real name is, was arrested in Baltimore for assault. The victim refused to press charges and the case was dismissed. The Mt. Clements possession charge you already know about."

"Interesting." I said. "It might be worth having another talk with Mr. Blackstone. Detective Bower, can you get the files on those cases sent to us ASAP?"

"Sure thing. I'll make the necessary calls after our meeting. Hopefully I can have them in a couple of days." Detective Bower responded.

"Ben, did you get a chance to talk to Mrs. Maxwell?" I asked.

"Not yet. I went by her house and she wasn't there. I went by her workplace and was told it was her day off. I did find out that she is working today, so I'm going to stop in and see her for lunch. I also obtained a search warrant for Kenny's apartment. Just say the word and we will go for it." Ben answered.

"Sounds good. But I want to hold off on executing that warrant until we get those files." I answered. "Let's get to work."

"Do you need me to take you to get a rental car?" Detective Bower asked gallantly.

"No, thanks Detective." I answered. "Jim's truck is in the garage and I have the keys so I'll just use that."

"God, don't get Jim's truck blown up. If the explosion doesn't kill you he will. You know how he feels about that truck." Ben said teasingly.

"Shut up Ben." I said laughing and throwing a pillow from the couch at him.

Bill's hammering of the drywall became increasingly loud, so we decided to break up the meeting. I gave everyone instructions to call me at home or on my cell phone as soon as they had anything.

Once everybody left, I made another pot of coffee and walked into my office to see how the repairs were coming along. Bill was making good progress and my several attempts at conversation failed. I guess he was still mad at me.

I went into my bedroom and after I shut the door, dialed Jim's number at the hospital. It was probably better that he heard what happened from me then from someone else. As I dialed his number I decided that the phone was too impersonal and he wouldn't believe I was okay unless he saw me anyway, so I decided just to go see him.

I gave Bill instructions on how to lock up the house and set the alarm. I opened the garage door and discovered that the tow truck was just backing into the driveway to take away the remains of my jeep. The crime scene crew had finished and was just leaving. The tow truck driver gave me a receipt for the truck and loaded it gingerly onto the flatbed. Then it was gone. I felt a deep sadness as I watched the tow truck pull out of the driveway. I had loved that jeep.

With a heavy sigh, I climbed into Jim's Durango and headed to the hospital.

I walked into Jim's room and was greeted with a weak but cheerful," Hi Savannah."

"Hey Jim. How are you feeling?" I asked gently.

"Better than I was. Boy am I glad to see you. I missed you." Jim said as he reached for my hand.

I pulled the chair up to his bed and took his hand in mine.

"I missed you too. Listen, I hope you don't mind if I drive your Durango for a couple of days." I said.

"No problem. Is your jeep in the shop?" Jim asked.

"In a matter of speaking." I responded evasively.

"What exactly does that mean?" Jim asked narrowing his eyes suspiciously.

"The jeep was involved in a little accident." I replied.

"What kind of accident? You're not hurt are you?" Jim asked concerned.

"No, I'm fine. I wasn't in the jeep at the time." I responded.

"What kind of accident was the jeep in?" Jim asked patiently.

"It kind of exploded." I said meekly.

"Exploded!" Jim said rising from the bed wincing in pain.

I took my hands and gently rested them on his shoulders easing him back down on the bed.

"Yeah. Judging from the explosion Marge thinks it was some type of pipe bomb." I said calmly.

"Why don't you tell me the whole story and let's save this game of twenty questions for when I'm feeling better, okay?" Jim asked with a slight edge to his voice.

"Okay." I said. I took a deep breath and filled him in on the investigation. Jim listened intently, asking a question or two now and then.

"So then your theory is that the killer blew up your jeep as your punishment for talking to the media. Is that right?" Jim asked.

"That's the best I can come up with right now." I answered.

"I think you're pushing him too hard Savannah. He's beginning to lose it." Jim said.

"I tend to agree, but I don't know exactly what I'm pushing. It seems to me that I am still being reactive and not proactive in this whole investigation. I need to figure out what buttons I'm pushing with this guy and use it to my advantage." I responded thoughtfully.

"Easier said than done." Jim said wryly. "You know this guy's profile better than anyone. Start there."

"I've been going over his profile every available minute." I said frustrated. "There just isn't anything there that is giving me the clue. The best I can figure is that he is frustrated because I'm not glorifying the killings in any way. I've been very careful to keep the sensationalism out of the media. Maybe that's what's making him go over the edge. What do you think?" I asked with genuine interest.

"I think you're right. I've seen the press conferences. You've done a remarkable job of keeping him out of the limelight and concentrating on the victims and yourself. That's bound to make him angry." Jim responded.

"Yes. He's not getting the attention he feels he deserves. That fits with his profile. I've probably frustrated him to no end." I said smugly.

"Question is, are you going to keep pushing him or give him what he wants to calm him down a little bit?" Jim asked, already knowing the answer.

"I'm going to push harder." I responded with determination, than added wryly, "Just as soon as I figure out what I'm going to push with."

"Just promise me two things." Jim said pleadingly.

"What's that?" I asked.

"Number one, promise me you'll be careful. Number two, promise me you won't destroy my truck." Jim said with a smile.

"You and that damn truck." I said laughing. "I promise I'll try."

"Coming from you that's one hell of a commitment." Jim said teasingly.

"Very funny." I retorted.

Jim and I spent the next hour or two chatting and watching TV. I went down to the gift shop and bought him some hunting magazines and snacks. When I left he was happily munching on M & M's and reading about the latest advancements in deer hunting techniques. A sport I never understood. Must be one of those guy things.

I got back home and found Bill applying the second coat of mud to the drywall in my office. He gave me a friendly wink as I walked in the office to grab my phone book. I settled in at the kitchen table and spent an hour or so finding a good mason to repair the brickwork on the outside of the house from the rifle shots. I found one who promised to stop by later this afternoon and take a look at the damage. So far so good.

I started to dial my insurance agent's home number but decided to hold off until tomorrow. Why mess up his only day off.

I had just hung up the phone when it rang. I answered it only to hear Clint's cheerful voice on the other end.

"Hi darlin." Clint said.

"Hi handsome." I responded cheerfully.

"I think I got something you'll be interested in." Clint said.

"Give it to me." I said expectantly.

"If the computer's correct, your killer has been a busy boy." Clint responded.

"Oh really?" I asked curiously.

"Listen, I'm not on a secure line here. Why don't I just fax you what I've got."

"Great. Fax away." I said laughing.

"You got it darlin. If you have any questions call me at the office tomorrow." Clint said, and then continued, "On a more serious note Savannah. I really have had to think twice about sending you some of this. Just promise me when you read it you won't let it send you into a tailspin."

"I promise." I answered pensively. "Why?"

My only response was a click on the other end of the phone as Clint hung up.

I heard the fax machine ring in my office and rushed in there to intercept the fax before Bill decided to get nosy. As the pages came through the fax I quickly skimmed through them. Then when I hit page seven, I let out an audible gasp and collapsed into my office chair allowing the pages in my hand to flutter to the floor.

CHAPTER 16

▼

"Savannah! Are you okay?" Bill asked rushing to my side.

"I'm fine." I said, pulling myself together. "I just wasn't expecting...I I've got to go."

I hastily picked up the papers I dropped on the floor and grabbed the remaining pages out of the fax machine.

"I don't think you should be going anywhere." Bill responded. "You're as white as a ghost. Just sit down and let me get you a glass of water."

"Make it wine. There's an open bottle in fridge." I yelled after Bill as he headed toward the kitchen.

Bill returned with my glass of wine and I took a hearty sip. My mind was racing two hundred miles per hour. I couldn't concentrate on a single thought.

"Okay," I told myself. "Calm down. Take a few deep breaths. You can't lose it now. That's it. Take another sip of wine. Good."

I came out of my thoughts to find Bill kneeling by my chair looking at me with deep concern written all over his face.

"Feel better?" Bill asked gently.

"Yes. Much." I said, making my voice sound stronger than I felt.

"Do you want me to call someone?" Bill asked.

"No. I'm fine. I just need to think about this for awhile." I responded.

The doorbell rang and Bill went to answer it. It was the brick mason I had called earlier.

"I'll talk to him Savannah. Why don't you just sit here and rest for awhile." Bill said.

"No, that's okay. I'll talk to him." I answered, happy to have a diversion.

I spent the next half hour or so discussing the brickwork that had to be done and after reaching an agreeable price, I gave him a deposit and he left promising to start the next day.

Feeling a lot better, I read through the fax that Clint had sent. The pieces of the puzzle were making sense now. I was very familiar with the killer I was dealing with. I just needed his name.

I quickly made a few phone calls and within minutes, Detective Bower, Detective Mitchell and Ben arrived at the house. We had a lot of work to do and not a lot of time to do it.

Bill continued to hover around me like a mother hen and I finally got Ben to chase him out of the house so we could get down to business.

Once everybody had retrieved something to drink out of the kitchen and had assembled in the great room I began.

"Okay. Here's what we've got. I received a fax from my contact in the FBI this afternoon. Our killer has struck before, five times in Baltimore and three times in Atlanta, Georgia. I want all of you to work on getting the files out of Baltimore and Atlanta. I want them here by Tuesday morning. In the meantime, I want Kenny's arrest records on my desk by tomorrow afternoon. The local police departments in Baltimore and Atlanta should cooperate. If they don't let me know and I will handle it. Any questions?" I stated looking at all of them.

They all nodded their heads in response.

"I think I remember hearing about those murders when I worked in Atlanta." Ben said thoughtfully. "I think the FBI came in and took over the investigation and that was the last I heard about it."

"Okay, then Ben you take the Atlanta murders. I have made copies of the fax from the FBI." I said distributing them. "I don't care how you divide them up, just do it. Report back to me as soon as you have something. Operate this from both sides. One of you work on getting the FBI files and another one of you concentrate on the local police agencies. I want every piece of paper both of them have. See if you can get them to fax the files today. If not, I want them Federal Expressed first thing in the morning. I'm going to work out some things from here. I have some old case files here from the Baltimore murders. Just so you'll know, judging from this fax, our killer is the same one that killed my ex-partner Frank."

"Are you okay Savannah?" Detective Bower asked.

"No. I'm not okay and I won't be okay until I nail this guy." I said firmly. "You all have your assignments. Let's get to work."

"Are you sure you don't want me to stay?" Detective Bower asked. "Maybe you shouldn't be alone right now."

"Detective Bower," I said sharply. "For your information I am not going to have another break down, at least not yet, I am not going to commit suicide and I do not need a babysitter. I am stronger, smarter and a whole lot more determined than I ever was. Now, all of you get out and get to work!"

Without another word all three of them hastily gathered their things and rushed out the door.

My nerves were shot and I felt that I was right on the edge of losing it. Determined not to let that happen I went into the kitchen and got a Valium out of my kitchen cabinet and downed it with another glass of wine. After retrieving my file on the Baltimore murders out of my safe in the basement, I headed into my office.

As I started to review the file I realized where my feelings of déjà vu had been coming from. The connection hadn't kicked in because the killer in Baltimore didn't use tarot cards, he used the symbols, but instead of putting them in a pentagram and using blood, he had simply carved a symbol into the forehead of his victim. Upon further review I discovered that the symbols in the Baltimore murders, instead of being looked at as some type of alphabet, had been assumed to be a counting system that the killer used to keep track of his victims.

I carefully transcribed the symbols onto a piece of paper from the photographs of the victims and put a call into Andy. I needed those books of his.

A few minutes later Andy called and said that his brother was getting married tonight, but he would be happy to drop off the books on the way to the church. I thanked him profusely and set aside the symbols. There were other things to consider.

I pulled out my profile from the current killings and compared them to my profile from the Baltimore murders. They were basically the same. I then thought about Kenny Blackstone. Number one he didn't fit the profile and number two I didn't think he was smart enough to plan and execute these types of murders. I knew I needed to have another chat with Mr. Blackstone once I had the files from the FBI.

I got up from the desk to stretch and grab a glass of wine from the kitchen. Just as I poured my wine the doorbell rang. It was Andy. He handed me the books and gave me his pager number in case I needed anything and took off.

I went back into the office and began to leaf through the books until I found the symbols I was looking for. They were from the Ogham alphabet, an ancient writing used by the Celtics peoples of Britain and Ireland. The symbols translated to S-A-V-A-N. It didn't take a rocket scientist to figure out that the killer was spelling my name, Savannah.

I sat back in my chair in dismay. This guy has been after me all along.

I began to pace around the house furious that this guy was using me as his catalyst to kill.

I went back into my office and flopped down in my chair. I lit a cigarette and watched the smoke dance around the room as it was gently blown by the breeze of the ceiling fan. It was time to get down to some serious thinking.

I looked at the dates of all the murders. I knew the Baltimore murders coincided with the dates I was in Baltimore. I was also in Atlanta at the time those murders took place, but hadn't been assigned to that case.

Another thing that bothered me was, assuming that the symbols left at the Atlanta murders spelled out the rest of my name, then why leave the tarot cards as clues in these murders and why warn the victim beforehand? Okay, I reasoned you have to warn the victims before you kill them because that's part of the game, that's how this guy gets off. Made sense. He's escalating the game, raising the stakes in a matter of speaking. He was playing the game of catch me if you can.

The dogs that came racing into the room full of energy interrupted my thoughts. I got up from my chair and let them out in the back yard. I wandered out on the deck and saw the car that had been parking behind the house sitting in the court with its lights off and engine running. Enough was enough. I quietly led the dogs back in the house and locked the doorwall. I grabbed my gun and went out the front door. This guy was mine.

I walked around the block and positioned myself behind the car using the partially built homes as cover. Keeping low, I cautiously crept along the driver side of the car. As I got closer to the front of the car I could hear soft music playing from his radio. That told me what I wanted to hear, his window was down. I softly crawled along side of the car until I got right underneath his window. I eased my gun out of the waist of my jeans and silently released the safety. Taking a deep breath I rose up and put the gun to his head.

"Don't even breath." I said firmly.

A look of total shock washed over the face of the man sitting in the car.

"I can explain." He said shakily.

"For your sake I certainly hope so." I replied. "I've had a really bad few weeks. I've been shot at, my dogs were fed sleeping pills, someone shot up my house, my ex-boyfriend has been shot, two people I know have been murdered, someone blew up my jeep, the press has been circling me like a pack of wolves and you've been watching my house for weeks." By the time I finished I was practically in tears. "Now," very slowly reach out and turn on the overhead lights of your car."

The man in the car reached out and flicked on the lights. I saw that he was young, maybe late twenties, short blond hair and the darkest eyes I had ever seen. He had a stocky build and was wearing faded blue jeans and a black button down cotton shirt. I saw a gun lying on the passenger seat next to him.

"Slowly, and I mean very slowly, reach your gun and hand it to me." I said softly.

His hand reached out and picked up the gun by the muzzle. He handed it to me and I tucked it in the waistband of my jeans.

"Good." I replied. "Now, why don't you tell me who you are and why you're watching my house."

"My name is Tom Clayton." He began in a deep, baritone voice. "I'm a private detective. I was hired by Mrs. Walker to see if you were having an affair with her husband."

"What!" I exclaimed in dismay. "You've got to be kidding."

"No, Ms. Williams. I never kid when I have a gun to my head." Tom said.

"Show me you're ID. Slowly." I responded.

Tom reached into his jean pocket and pulled out his wallet. He opened it up to show me his private detective license.

I took the gun away from his head and put it back on safety. I reached behind me and handed him back his gun. I could see the relief wash over his face.

"Well, Tom." I said with a smile." You've got a lot to learn about surveillance. Why would Mrs. Walker hire you to watch me? I know she didn't see me when I followed her."

"A friend of Mrs. Walker's saw you and her husband together at the Log Cabin Restaurant a few weeks ago and mentioned it to Mrs. Walker. She assumed you were having an affair and hired me. I guess her husband travels a lot for his job and she thought that some of the business trips were bogus and that he was really with you." Tom explained.

"I met Mr. Walker at the restaurant because he hired me to find out if his wife was having an affair." I said.

"So you mean," Tom said starting to giggle, "that I have spent the last few weeks watching you watching her?"

"Yes." I said, both of us laughing. "Listen, you've wasted a lot of time. Why don't you give me a lift to my house so I can grab my bag and I'll buy you dinner and a couple of beers?"

"That would be great." Tom responded and then teasingly said, "Maybe you could give me some tips on surveillance why we're eating.

"You need all the help you can get." I said sliding into the passenger side of his car.

"Someone really blew up your jeep?" Tom asked incredulously.

"Yes, the second one in three years. My insurance agent is either going to kill me or commit suicide." I said wryly.

With a laugh, Tom put the car in gear and drove me to my house. I ran in and fed the dogs and retrieved my purse. We then headed down to the Stop Light Tavern to get some dinner. I was starving.

I waved to Bobby and Russ as we walked in. Instead of sitting at the bar like I usually did, Tom and I decided to grab a table by the bar. It would be more private and we would have more room to eat.

We each ordered a big steak with all trimmings. Tom ordered a beer and I ordered a glass of white zin. Once the waitress brought our drinks we started to chat about the private detective business.

I found out that Tom had only had his license for six months. He had been a cop in nearby Port Huron and had been injured in the line of duty. He left the force and decided to become a private detective. I was surprised to learn that he was really thirty-three and not in his twenties.

Our food arrived and we ordered another round of drinks with dinner. We spent the next twenty minutes or so in silence, both of us concentrating on the excellent food placed in front of us. Finally, we sat back totally stuffed, but satisfied. I drained the last of my wine and as I did so, I noticed a small blinking red light coming from the top corner of the bar area. I hadn't noticed it before, but if your sitting at the bar you wouldn't be able to see it.

"Oh shit." I said in shock and disbelief.

"What?" Tom asked looking around.

"I'll be right back." I said rising from the table.

I walked over to the bar and flagged down Barb.

"Barb, what's that blinking light up there?" I asked pointing up to the corner of the ceiling behind the bar.

"Oh, that's the security camera." Barb replied nonchalantly, and then, realizing the significance of the question said, "Oh my God."

"My thought exactly." I replied and then asked, "Barb, do you have the tapes from that machine for the nights Mr. Maxwell and Matt were in here before they were murdered?"

"Yes. They must be in the back. We date each tape and use a new tape each day. You don't think the killer might be on those tapes do you? Oh Savannah, I'm so sorry, I didn't even think of the security camera, no one really pays any attention to it." Barb asked.

"It's okay Barb. I never even thought to ask. I need those tapes. I want the tapes. Can you get them for me." I said, not bothering to answer her question.

"I'll have to talk to the manager. Hang on." Barb said and quickly disappeared into an office along side the bar.

Barb re-emerged a few minutes later with two tapes in her hand.

"The manager said you could have them and if you need anything else, just to let him know. He said just to bring them back when you're finished with them." Barb said.

"Thanks Barb." I said warmly. "I owe you one."

"Just get that guy." Barb said firmly.

"I promise." I said somberly.

I returned to the table and put the tapes in my bag.

"What are those for?" Tom asked curiously.

I quickly explained everything to Tom.

"So, how about if we go back to your place, I'll make some popcorn and we'll catch ourselves a killer." Tom said when I had finished.

I nodded in agreement and after paying the bill, we made a hasty retreat from the restaurant.

CHAPTER 17

▼

We arrived at the house and while I let the dogs out, Tom rummaged around the kitchen making popcorn. He was serious!

We settled in on the couch with popcorn and beer and put the tape of the night Mr. Maxwell into the VCR. We fast-forwarded through it until we saw Mr. Maxwell come into the bar.

We watched in silence as he sat down and began talking to Matt, Bobby and Russ.

The camera must be programmed to pivot, because it kept panning around the bar in timed intervals. As the camera scanned around the bar and restaurant, I finally caught sight of Kenny coming in the door. He took a seat at a table by the bar with a few other men who looked like they might have been construction workers.

After a while, Matt, Bobby and Russ left and Mr. Maxwell was sitting at the bar alone. He ordered another beer. In the background I saw Kenny's friends leave the bar and Kenny come over to the bar and sit a chair away from Mr. Maxwell. They soon struck up a conversation. A little while later Mr. Maxwell left the bar with Kenny right behind him. I turned off the tape at that point.

"What do you think?" Tom asked. "Is that your guy?"

"I don't know." I responded pensively. "It certainly seems that way, but he doesn't fit the profile."

"Maybe your profile is wrong." Tom said glibly as he took another swig of beer.

"My profile is not wrong." I said defensively. "This killer is highly intelligent, highly organized and very familiar with police procedures. Kenny just doesn't strike me as being very intelligent or organized. I'll admit that my profile may need to be tweaked a little bit, but it is not that far off. I just don't know."

"Maybe if we watch the other tape it will help." Tom said.

"Can't hurt." I responded as I rose from the couch to change the tapes. "I just can't help but feel that I've missed something important."

Tom pressed the play button and the bar soon came into view on the television screen.

Tom and I watched the second tape in silence. There was no sign of Kenny in the second tape. Not surprising.

Tom flipped off the tape and took the empty popcorn bowl into the kitchen.

"So what are you going to tell Mrs. Walker?" I asked curiously.

"I'm not sure. Any suggestions" Tom asked smiling.

"How about the truth." I responded.

"Could work." Tom said thoughtfully. "So, is Mrs. Walker having an affair?"

"I don't know." I admitted. "I followed her to a restaurant just outside of Algonac. She met a man there, but they left separately. They had an intense conversation, but they didn't look like lovers to me."

"What did this guy look like?" Tom asked.

"I'll show you his picture. Come into the office." I said.

Tom followed me into the office and I pulled out my file on Mrs. Walker. Tom studied the picture and then said. "That's her brother."

"Are you sure?" I asked.

"Positive. He was at her house when I went there for the initial consultation. Mr. Walker and Mrs. Walker's brother do not get along. That's why she only sees him when Mr. Walker is out of town." Tom answered.

"So," I asked casually, "why did you follow me the night I followed Mrs. Walker? It was obvious I was alone."

"I didn't follow you. I've never followed you. I know you live alone and if you and Mr. Walker were going to meet, your house would be the logical place." Tom answered.

"That's strange." I said. "So if it wasn't you, it had to be the killer."

"Probably." Tom said. "Listen, do you want me to stay and sleep on the couch tonight?"

"That's probably not a good idea." I answered. "The last guy that slept on the couch was shot."

"I see your point." Tom said easing his way to the door. "I'll just be going now."

"Cute." I said walking him to the door. "Just remember, if you get any tarot cards in the mail, call me." I said with a wink.

"Not even funny Savannah." Tom said as he left.

I let the dogs out one more time and then locked all the doors, set the alarm and went to bed. No doubt about it. Another long talk with Kenny was definitely in the cards. Pardon the pun.

I woke up at five, took a quick shower and got dressed. While I was having my morning coffee, I called Detective Bower and told him to call a press conference for nine-thirty and to meet me in the conference room at the police station at nine o'clock. I then called Ben, Marge and Cal and told them to meet me in the conference room at nine. After that I phoned Detective Marshall and told him to bring in Kenny no earlier than nine fifteen.

I called Jim at the hospital and updated him on the case. I was bringing Kenny in. I honestly didn't think that Kenny was the killer, but I needed a button to push with the real killer. This was it.

Feeling guilty for neglecting the dogs, I put them on their leashes and headed for the woods. Once we were in the woods I set them free to roam around. They darted through the trees yapping and barking in glee. I sat down in the middle of the clearing where Matt's body was found and formulated my plans for the day. Timing was going to be everything.

Coming out of my thoughts, I glanced at my watch. It was eight fifteen. I called the dogs and led them home. After they ate a hearty breakfast, I took them out into the backyard and we played catch.

As I was just backing out of the driveway, the brick mason showed up and after a brief discussion he began working on the house. I headed for the police station stopping only for a cup of coffee on my way.

I got to the police station and found a stack of mail waiting for me at the front desk. Having no time to go through it, I took it into the conference room with me and joined the rest of the team.

Everyone was there with the exception of Detective Marshall and I knew where he was.

Just as I was about to begin, the Desk Sergeant stuck his head in the conference room door and said I had a phone call.

I picked up the phone.

"This is Savannah Williams. May I help you?"

"Hi Ms. Williams. This is Detective Marshall."

"What's up Detective?" I asked impatiently.

"I'm at Kenny's apartment." Detective Marshall said.

"Great. Do you need back-up?" I asked.

" No Ma'am. I need a Crime Scene Unit. I don't know quite how to tell you this Ms. Williams. Kenny is dead."

"What!" I exclaimed jumping to my feet. "What do you mean he's dead? Are you sure?"

"Yes Ma'am. Quite sure. I'm sorry Ms. Williams." Detective Marshall answered.

"Hang on a second Detective. I'm going to put you on speaker." I said. "Okay people we have a problem. Kenny Blackstone has just turned up dead and we have a press conference in fifteen minutes. Cal and Marge, you head to the scene and begin processing it. Don't, I repeat, don't touch the body until I get there. Detective Marshall, I need you to seal off the scene. Nobody goes in or out except for Cal and Marge. Detective Bower, you get out there and help Detective Marshall until the black and whites get there. Got that people?"

"Yes Ma'am." Everybody responded.

"Ben, head out to the scene. I'll meet you there. On the way out, have a couple of marked units sent to the scene to help lock it down. Let's roll." I said rising from table after getting the address from Detective Marshall and hanging up the phone.

"What about the press conference?" Ben asked.

"The Chief will have to handle it." I said.

Cal, Marge, Detective Bower and Ben raced out of the room to gather their equipment and head to the scene.

I padded down the hall and up the stairs to the Chief's office. I tapped on the door and was told to enter.

The Chief was sitting behind a massive desk that dwarfed his huge frame. Something I didn't think was possible.

"What is it Savannah?" The Chief asked, distracted by some paperwork on his desk.

"I have a bit of a logistics problem I need you to solve for me." I said tactfully.

"What kind of a logistics problem?" The Chief asked suspiciously.

"Well, you see, Sir, it's like this." I began apprehensively, "Detective Marshall just called in and is with Kenny." I started to explain.

"Good. That's great, but I still fail to see the problem." The Chief said.

"If you would let me finish Sir." I said meekly. "The problem is this. Kenny is dead. I have everyone on the way to the crime scene and I need to join them. There is a press conference in five minutes. I need you to cover that for me."

"What the hell am I supposed to say at this press conference?" the Chief asked. I could tell he was becoming quite agitated.

"I'm not really sure Sir. I guess you'll just have to punt." I said with a wicked smile as I leapt out of the chair and escaped out the door. I could hear his booming voice yelling my name as I bounded down the stairs from his office and raced out the front door. I jumped into my Jim's Durango and lit up the tires as I headed toward Kenny's apartment.

CHAPTER 18

▼

I arrived at the scene and was directed to a first floor apartment by one of the uniformed officers on the scene. Detective Marshall was standing outside the door to Kenny's apartment.

I opened the door to Kenny's apartment and entered. I assumed Detective Marshall was right behind me. I was wrong. I stuck my head out of the door to the apartment.

"Coming Detective Marshall?" I asked, noticing that he was a little green around the gills.

"Yes Ma'am." Detective Marshall said slowing moving inside the door of the apartment. "Does it ever get easier?" he asked miserably.

"No Detective," I responded, "it doesn't get easier. You just get used to death. After your third or fourth murder scene you become numb."

"Gee, that gives me something to look forward to." Detective Marshall said sarcastically.

I ignored his remark and looked around the living room of Kenny's apartment. The crime scene personnel were dusting for fingerprints so I was careful not to touch anything. A second hand black vinyl couch, an old television, two cheap end tables each with a lamp that didn't have lampshades were the only furniture in the room. Newspapers and hunting magazines were on a glass-topped coffee table in front of the couch along with a glass that contained some kind of liquid. After seeing all there was to see in there I moved into the kitchen.

Fast food wrappers and pizza boxes were strewn around the counters and dirty dishes were stacked high in the sink. Beer cans were stacked in a pyramid on the small, fake wood kitchen table. Two folding chairs were around the kitchen table and were draped with various items of clothing.

I left the kitchen and wandered down the short hallway to the bedroom. Cal and Marge were in the bedroom along with one of the police photographers who was snapping pictures of the scene.

"Hi Ms. Williams." The photographer said with a smile. "I'm almost finished here. I have already videotaped the entire apartment, I just wanted to get some still shots."

"Take your time." I responded and moved into the room to survey the scene.

Kenny was lying on a mattress that was on the floor with a tarot card stabbed into his chest. I bent over and looked at the card. The card showed a picture of a woman sitting up in bed crying. Above the bed, horizontally were nine swords. The card was the Nine of Swords. Kenny was dressed in a pair of black socks, faded blue jeans and black T-shirt. His eyes were closed and he had a rather peaceful look on his face. I looked carefully at his wrists and saw the same type of marks that were left on Matt and Mr. Maxwell. The pillow under his head was soaked in blood.

Across from the bed painted on the wall with black spray paint was the pentagram. There were different symbols written in blood. They were a little hard to make out because some of the blood had run down the wall and merged with other symbols. It really didn't matter. I knew what they meant. This was number three.

I walked over to the dresser on the wall next to the bed. Lying on top of the dresser was another tarot card sticking out of a manila envelope. I borrowed a pair of latex gloves from Marge and examined the envelope. There was no postmark. I gently eased the card out of the envelope. The card showed a man lying face down on the ground with ten swords piercing his body. It was the Ten of Swords. It was glued onto a piece of cardboard right side up.

I gave Marge and Cal the go ahead to process the scene and left the bedroom. I ducked into the bathroom. You can always tell a lot about a person by what they keep in their medicine cabinet.

Kenny's medicine cabinet told a sad story. There was a half empty tube of toothpaste, a toothbrush, razor, shave cream, comb, and a half full bottle of antacid. Dirty towels littered the floor. The shower only held a bar of soap and shampoo. It was a sad scene and I was totally depressed as I walked back out into the bedroom.

Pulling myself together, I walked over to Detective Marshall who was leaning weakly against one of the walls.

"Detective Marshall," I asked, trying to take his mind off the gory scene in front of us, "What's missing?"

"Excuse me?" Detective Marshall asked.

"What's missing from this scene that was present at the other ones?" I asked patiently.

"I don't understand." Detective Marshall said pensively.

"Detective. If you are going to continue to work in homicide, you need to emotionally remove yourself from what is in front of you and look at the scene logically and with detachment. I can spot three very important differences between this scene and the others. You have studied all the files on this case. Tell me what they are." I said, goading him into action.

Detective Marshall slowly walked around Kenny's bedroom looking at everything and examining a few items. After his tour of the room he came over and stood in front of me.

"Well," he began, "for one thing there isn't a dead animal. So where did the killer get the blood used to make the symbols?"

"Excellent. That's one." I said encouragingly.

"The envelope that the tarot card was in isn't postmarked. So the killer must have brought it to the scene." Detective Marshall said warming up to his subject.

"Okay, and the third?" I asked.

"Judging from the scene. Kenny was killed here. The other victims were killed elsewhere and carefully placed where they were found." Detective Marshall said finishing with a flourish.

"Good work Detective." I responded heartily. "Now, what does that tell you about our killer?"

"He's becoming desperate. He's starting to lose it mentally and emotionally. We are pushing him too hard, getting to close. For what is probably the first time in his killing career he is scared that he is going to get caught."

"Exactly." I said with a sly smile.

"So who is our killer? With Kenny dead we don't have anything?" Detective Marshall asked.

"That's not quite true. To quote Sir Arthur Conan Doyle in *The Sign of Four*, 'when you have eliminated the impossible, whatever remains, however improbable, must be the truth.' Think about it Detective." I said mysteriously as I turned away from him and walked over to talk to Cal.

"What have you got so far?" I asked Cal.

"Well, so far we know that like the others he was probably unconscious before he was killed. There's a small entry wound in the side of the head, not unlike the other victims, probably killed with the same gun. This time however, the killer didn't have time to plan for an animal so he made a slit in the back of his victim's neck and drained the blood from the jugular vein to use to make the symbols in the pentagram. I would put the time of death somewhere between eight and ten o'clock last night." Cal finished.

"Good work Cal. When you're ready you can take the body." I responded. I wandered into the kitchen and started poking through cupboards and drawers. I opened the refrigerator and saw a carton of eggs, a package of bologna, beer and a loaf of stale bread.

I told Ben and Detectives Bower and Marshall that they could leave. I would hang around and wait until everyone was finished. I wanted them to go back to the station and work on getting those files. I wanted them faxed to my house by this afternoon.

It was well after noon before I got out of Kenny's apartment. I made sure that the door was securely sealed and then threatened the manager with certain death if he let anyone in or out of there without checking with me first.

On my way home I called my insurance agent and told him about my jeep exploding and where it had been towed. He listened patiently, said they would pay the claim and berated me about my line of work. I thanked him for his concern over my well being and drove to a Dodge dealership to pick out a new vehicle.

After carefully looking over all the vehicles on the lot, I decided on a black Jeep Grand Cherokee. It was awesome. It had dark gray leather heated seats, a sunroof, four-wheel drive and a six CD changer. It was definitely my kind of truck.

I signed the purchase order, filled out a ton of paperwork and gave the salesman the name and number of my insurance agent to work out the rest of the details. I arranged to pick it up the next day.

After a quick stop at Madame Phoebe's to buy a deck of tarot cards, I headed home.

I pulled up to the house to find Sandra's BMW parked in the driveway. I said hello to Sandra who was busy dishing up Chinese food in the kitchen.

"So what's up?" Sandra asked.

"The killer blew up my jeep." I stated flatly.

"He what?!" Sandra screamed in dismay.

"He blew up my jeep. Thank God for that auto start or I would have gone up with it." I replied gratefully as I gathered silverware and napkins and placed them on the table.

"Land sakes alive!" Sandra exclaimed as she walked over to me and gave me a big hug. "You were almost killed. What are you going to do?"

"Be more careful." I said shrugging my shoulders. "What else can I do? I'm not going to back off. I'm too close. A few more days and I should have this guy cold."

"A few more days and you could be dead." Sandra retorted.

"Not a chance." I responded with a wink. "Only the good die young."

"Do you know who the killer is?" Sandra asked totally ignoring my attempt at humor.

"I think I know what he is, but not who he is. Hopefully I'll have some answers by late this afternoon." I answered mysteriously.

"What do you mean?" Sandra asked mystified.

"I mean just what I said." I responded evasively. "So are you ready for your presentation?

Realizing that she wasn't going to pry any more information out of me, Sandra gave up and told me about her marketing presentation she had this afternoon.

Sandra and I ate lunch and then she had to rush off. I walked her to the door and gave her a big hug for luck.

After she had left, I let the dogs out and finished cleaning up the kitchen. I then sat down with the pile of mail that had been delivered to the police station.

Most of the mail was either fan letters or threatening letters. Typical. I then came to a manila envelope at the bottom of the stack. There was no post-mark. I instinctively knew it was from the killer.

I quickly ran to the phone and called the police station and asked to talk to Ben. I was told he was out of the station, but Detective Bower was there. I was put through to Detective Bower and told him to grab an evidence kit and get over to my house. The one I had checked out of the police station unfortunately had gone up in flames with my jeep.

While I was waiting for Detective Bower, I looked up the cards left at the scene of Kenny's murder. The Nine of Swords roughly meant cruelty, misery, lying dishonesty. The Ten of Swords meant misfortune, burdens to bear. It could also mean ruin, pain, utter defeat or the death of a loved one.

Upon reading that, I immediately dialed Jim's number at the hospital.

"Hello." Jim answered. His voice sounded stronger.

"Hi. It's me." I said. "Are you okay?"

"Yeah, I'm fine. Why?" Jim responded.

I explained to him what had happened to Kenny and the meaning of the tarot cards left at the scene.

"I was just concerned. I thought maybe the killer was coming after you." I said relieved.

"Not yet." Jim answered glibly. "Ben is here and we are just talking shop. Do you need to talk to him?"

"No. So, I was thinking," I began shyly, "when the doctor releases you from the hospital, maybe you should stay here awhile until you get your strength back."

"I'll think about it. Thanks." Jim responded emotionlessly.

"Fine. I'll talk to you later." I said put off and slammed the phone back into the receiver.

I didn't even have time to fume about my conversation with Jim before Detective Bower showed up at the door.

I let him in and we each donned a pair of gloves from the evidence kit. With an exacto knife I slit open the envelope and slowly slid out the piece of cardboard inside. Glued to the cardboard was a tarot card. It was the Magician. I ran into the office and looked up the card in the tarot book. Since the card was reversed, it meant the use of power for destructive ends.

"Do you have any idea what this all means?" Detective Bower asked.

"Yes. It means that I am next." I replied simply, tossing the card aside.

"He's coming after you?" Detective Bower asked incredulously.

"Sure is. The game has just escalated. Now it's a game of kill or be killed." I responded firmly.

"I won't let him get to you." Detective Bower said fiercely.

"You don't have to worry about that Detective. I'm going to make him come to me at a time and place of my choosing." I said confidently. "Its my move."

"How are you going to do that?" Detective Bower asked mystified. "You don't even know who this guy is."

"I'm beginning to Detective." I responded thoughtfully. "Try this on for size. What if our killer is a cop?"

"One of our own?" Detective Bower asked in disbelief.

"Think about it." I said. "This guy has been one step ahead of us this whole investigation. He knows every move we are going to make before we make it and can compensate for it."

"That does make sense." Detective Bower responded doubtfully. "But I still fail to see how it all ties together."

"Well, let's look at what we know." I said leaning back in my chair and lighting a cigarette. "First, we know that this killer is the same one that is responsible for other deaths in other cities. We know that this guy has some obsession or connection with me. We also know that I have pushed this guy to the limit. I haven't given him the notoriety in the press. That's his trigger. He wants to be noticed, he wants to read about himself in the papers and see himself on the nightly news. We haven't given him that. The only reason Kenny was murdered is because we were going to charge him with the murders and take the spotlight off the real killer."

"So our killer is an egomaniac." Detective Bower said.

"Exactly, but not outwardly. Now we just have to figure out who." I said ruefully.

"Well, you obviously don't think its me or you wouldn't have shared this information." Detective Bower began. "We can eliminate

Marge, because our killer is male. Jim is out for obvious reasons. That leaves us with Detective Mitchell, Ben or a cop on the force."

"I think we can eliminate Detective Mitchell. He can't even look at a murder scene without barfing his guts up." I said laughing.

"Okay. So that leaves us with Ben or a cop on the force." Detective Bower stated. "What do you need me to do?"

"I need you to go to the station and get me a copy of the report concerning the night my house was broken into and the dogs were drugged. I also need you to pick up any new reports from Marge and bring them back here along with a list of every cop on the force that worked in Baltimore and Atlanta at the time of the previous murders. Oh, and I hope you don't have any plans for tonight, its going to be a long one."

"Okay, but I don't like this. I mean a cop. Come on Savannah, are you sure?" Detective Bower asked dejectedly.

I got up from my chair and put my hands on Detective Bower's broad shoulders.

"I don't like it either Mark, but sometimes this job requires us to do a lot we don't like. A lot of innocent people have died at the hands of this monster, including Frank. I owe him this. Do you understand?" I asked pleadingly. I could feel tears welling up in my eyes and I fought hard to hold them back.

"You are a remarkable woman Savannah." Detective Bower said, wrapping me in a hug. "I'll never understand how Jim could let you go."

I eased myself out of the hug.

"I do believe that is the nicest thing you've ever said to me." I responded wiping the tears out of my eyes. "Now get out of here. I hate mushy scenes. I'm going to go to the hospital and lay this all out for Jim and get his opinion. Meet me back here in two hours."

"Okay. See you then, and Savannah, be careful." Detective Bower said heading for the front door.

"Always." I said with a wink as I opened the door for him. "Always."

CHAPTER 19

▼

Once Detective Bower left I called and spoke briefly with the Chief, He was still pretty sore at me for dumping the press conference on him, but once I laid out my theory he agreed to give Detective Bower a copy of anything he needed.

"I hope to God you're wrong, Savannah." Chief said sadly.

"So do I Chief. More than you know." I responded.

"Maybe I could talk to some of the guys, sort of feel them out." The Chief offered.

"If it was only that easy. Unfortunately all we have is circumstantial evidence. We need more. I'm going to get it and the only way to do that is to make him come after me." I answered.

"I'm not sure I am prepared to let you take that risk, Savannah." The Chief said pensively. "You better come up with another way."

"There is no other way Chief you know I'm right about this." I said firmly. "When the time comes, I will call you and arrange for appropriate backup. Okay?"

"As long as you promise me you won't go after him alone. I guess that's the best compromise we can come up with." The Chief agreed. "What's your next step?"

"Well, first I'm going to go to the hospital and talk to Jim. Then I'm going to set the trap." I said evasively.

"What kind of trap?" The Chief asked.

"I'm going to send the killer a tarot card, in a matter of speaking." I answered quietly.

"Your what?! The Chief asked confused. "Are you out of your mind?"

"I don't think so." I answered with mock seriousness.

"Okay. We'll play this your way, but I don't like it. Make sure you keep in touch." The Chief responded apprehensively.

"Sure thing. Talk to you later." I answered and hung up the phone.

I locked up the house and drove to the hospital to see Jim. I walked into his room to find him up and walking around the hospital room.

"What are you doing?" I asked incredulously.

"Savannah! Just the person I wanted to see. I'm just getting a little exercise." Jim answered with a big goofy grin.

"Are you sure you're strong enough?"

"I'm sure, you worry wart." Jim said as he took his hand and mussed my hair. "After a few days of rest I'll be good as new. So, what's up?"

"Let's get you back in bed first and we'll talk there." I answered evasively.

"There's been a break in the case hasn't there?" Jim asked.

He always could see through me.

"Yes." I answered simply not able to look him in the eye.

"Okay. Let's hear it." Jim said after getting himself rearranged in bed.

I spent the next hour laying out the case for him. I went over everything I knew and what I assumed. Jim listened carefully and without interruption. That was certainly a first. After I finished, I sat back in the chair quietly to give him a few minutes to absorb all the information.

"I just can't believe it's a cop." Jim said shaking his head.

"I know. I had a hard time believing it too." I said sympathetically.

"I assume you have a plan in place?" Jim asked curiously.

"In a manner of speaking" I responded evasively as I refilled Jim's glass with ice water and set it back on the table next to the bed.

"Let's hear it." Jim said wearily.

"Well, it's still in the planning stages. I haven't worked out all of the details yet, but my first step is to send the killer a tarot card." I answered.

"Don't you think you might be pushing him just a little too far Savannah?" Jim asked quietly.

"I thought about that." I answered truthfully. "But no, given the circumstances, I don't think so. He is coming after me anyway as indicated by the tarot card he sent me.

"I see your point." Jim responded thoughtfully. "It would be a more controllable situation that way. At least we will know he is coming."

"Yes, and I will be ready for him." I said with more confidence then I felt.

"Hey, listen, not to change the subject, but do you think you could call for a ride and leave my truck here? The doctor said he is going to release me maybe as early as tomorrow and with all that is going on it would just be easier." Jim asked.

"Sure, no problem." I said, picking up the phone.

I called Detective Bower at the police station and arranged to have him pick me up at the hospital on his way back over to my house. That done I said goodbye to Jim and went downstairs to wait for Detective Bower. While I was waiting I called the car dealership and learned that I could take delivery of my new truck.

Detective Bower arrived right on time and drove me to the dealership to get my truck.

We arrived back at the house and settled in the office to review the paperwork Detective Bower had retrieved from the police station.

I started with the police report from the night the dogs were drugged. The report showed that the only fingerprints found at the scene besides mine were all accounted for. All that told me was that I knew the killer and he had been invited into my house, or he had worn gloves.

The next half hour was spent in complete silence as Detective Bower and I scoured the case files and miscellaneous reports.

Detective Marshall called from the police station and said that some of the reports from the FBI had just arrived by Federal Express. I told him to sit tight and Detective Bower would be right there to pick them up.

Detective Bower left for the station and I sat back down to review the tapes from the Stop Light Tavern again. I had missed something. I could feel it.

Instead of fast forwarding the tapes to the point Mr. Maxwell and Kenny entered the restaurant, I watched the tape from the beginning. As I watched the tape another familiar figure entered the bar. Stopping the tape, I quickly inserted the tape of the night Matt was murdered.

It only took about ten minutes to find what I was looking for.

"Gotcha." I whispered, clicking off the VCR. I knew who the killer was, now I just had to prove it.

Detective Bower returned a few minutes later with the Baltimore and Atlanta case files that the FBI had sent. Knowing I had to work fast, I attacked the files with newfound determination. It didn't take long for me to find what I was looking for. The fingerprints of the killer were everywhere, but because he was a cop on the scene, there was no reason to suspect him and his fingerprints were automatically set aside without question. Understandable, I had done the same thing with the police report from the night the dogs were drugged.

After sending Detective Bower home I set my plan into action.

I carefully went through the tarot cards that I had purchased from Madame Phoebes and looked up their meanings in the tarot card book the killer had sent me. How ironic.

The card I finally decided on was the Tower. Upside down or reversed, the card meant oppression, imprisonment.

I flipped on my computer and after carefully selecting just the right font and type size, entered the following message to the killer:

> Know who you are.
>
> Game over. I win.
>
> Savannah

I then formatted the page so that the first sentence of my message appeared at the top of the page. I left room for the tarot card to be glued in the center of the page and then the second sentence at the bottom of the page. I printed out the page and carefully glued the tarot card in place. I sat back pleased with the results.

I spent the next half hour or so placing calls to the editors of the newspapers in the area. All the editors agreed to print the card and the message in tomorrow's newspaper.

The rest of the day I was busy dropping off copies of the print for the papers and putting together what evidence I had against the killer, which was mostly circumstantial, but would have to do for now.

I didn't have the heart to go see Jim and fill him in. Maybe it was that I didn't have the guts, I don't know. But I also knew that if I told Jim he would order the murderer picked up right away and that is not how I wanted this to play out. I wanted the confrontation. No. I needed the confrontation. I had to come face to face with the man who gunned down Frank and almost destroyed my life. I was owed at least that much.

CHAPTER 20

▼

Looking back, I am surprised at the eerie sense of calm I felt the morning of the confrontation. It was almost over. The last two years of pure unadulterated hell were finally going to end. Maybe I would finally be able to close the gaping wound Frank's death had left in my heart. Maybe I would finally find some peace.

"Huh," I spoke out loud, "maybe I would end up dead."

Pushing all thoughts of that possibility aside, I began my preparations for the day to come. I showered and chose my clothes with care. I donned a pair of baggy jeans and oversized black T-shirt. I left my hair loose and after drying it straight, it fell just below the waistband of my jeans. Perfect.

The phone began ringing off the hook at eight o'clock that morning.

Jim called and demanded to know just what in blue blazes I was thinking. I hung on him.

The Chief called and in not so many nice words read me the riot act. I suppose I deserved that. I apologized profusely for not filling him in earlier. I also told him that back up would be not only needed, but greatly appreciated, with the condition that they were to stay out of sight until needed. He begrudgingly agreed to that stipulation.

Within an hour or so after talking to the Chief the partially finished houses behind mine became a flurry of activity. The normal construction crew that had been working on the houses had been joined by undercover police officers.

The neighbors two doors down were getting their outside windows washed courtesy of Ashley's finest, and the power company seemed to have a lot of repairs to make at one of the transformers on a light post on the corner. A Federal Express truck pulled up in my driveway and delivered an envelope. Inside was a small voice activated tape recorder and small wireless microphone complements of the Chief.

I checked to make sure the tape recorder was working and placed it and the microphone on top of the big screen television well out of sight in a basket of fake ivy. Excellent, everything was in place. Shouldn't be enough to scare him off, but I was a little concerned just the same. Nothing could possibly go wrong. Yeah right.

I had a hunch I wouldn't have to wait long for the killer to show up, so I had to make sure I was ready for any possibility.

I went down to the basement and unlocked the safe. I extracted a small caliber pistol and ankle holster. After loading the gun, I strapped it into place on my right ankle and practiced drawing it a few times to make sure the motion was fluid and quick. My life could depend on it.

Turning my attention back to the safe I withdrew another gun and after making sure the clip was loaded, snapped it into place in the butt of the gun. That I tucked into the back waistband of my jeans, along with my trusty Beretta. A girl can never be too prepared you know.

I went back upstairs and poured a cup of coffee and retreated to my office. I stared out the newly installed bay windows thinking about the last two years of my life. I thought about all that had been taken from me due to this one man. I thought about how much I hated him and yet pitied him at the same time. Most of all I tried to figure out why.

I gave the dogs huge rawhide bones that they happily took into my bedroom to eat. I heard the sound of the water swishing around as they settled in on the waterbed with their treat.

I saw his truck pull in my driveway. I watched as he got out of the truck and cautiously scanned the street for any sign of the police. Seemingly satisfied that all was as it should be, I watched as he walked up the front porch steps and rang the doorbell. Show time.

Taking a deep breath I opened the door and looked him right in the eye, searching for something, remorse fear, all I saw was hate.

"Come in Ben." I said quietly as I backed away from the door to let him enter.

Ben walked through the door and purposely shut it behind him, his eyes never leaving mine.

Perhaps he was looking for something too. Something he obviously didn't find.

Ben walked by me, drew his gun, and searched the house. Satisfied that I was alone, he turned his attention back to me.

"When did you figure it all out?" He asked simply.

"Yesterday." I answered, never taking my eyes off the gun he held so casually in his hand.

"Give me your gun Savannah." Ben said firmly, as he pointed his gun at my chest.

Having no choice, I reached in the waistband of my jeans and handed him my Beretta.

"Now walk." Ben said, waving the gun toward the kitchen.

I walked into the kitchen with Ben close behind me. Once we reached the kitchen, Ben motioned me into a chair at the kitchen table. He obviously was in no rush. Neither was I.

I watched as Ben poured himself a glass of whiskey and me a glass of wine. I paid close attention to make sure he did not drug my wine. He didn't. He wordlessly walked over and set the wine in front of me on the table.

Pulling out a chair for himself, he sat facing me at the table. There was nothing between us now and I did not like how close he was. I would have no time to draw a gun and fire at this close range. I had to find a way to get further away from him.

"I wish it had not come to this Savannah, but you gave me no other choice." Ben began.

Before I could stop them tears welled up in my eyes and began to roll down my face. I was finally going to get some answers. I took a sip of wine to steady my nerves and give me a second to think.

"You had a choice Ben. You had lots of choices. Every time you set out to kill another innocent person, you had a choice." I lashed out viciously.

"No I didn't Savannah, it was the only way I could get your attention. I tried to get you to back off when you were getting too close, but you didn't listen to me." Ben snapped back.

"What?" I asked incredulously. "You did this for my attention?"

Even the thought made me furious beyond belief.

"Of course I did Savannah." Ben responded angrily. "I'm not a killer. You know that. But the only way I could be close to you was to draw you into another case. Make it irresistible to you. The only way to do that was to kill. You made the choice Savannah, not I."

"But all those innocent people Ben" I said sadly. "Why all those innocent people?"

"You never gave me the time of day Savannah. You and the damn men you chose to associate with. They were all wrong for you. They didn't understand you the way I do. Jim, now that was a mistake, he thought he could tame you, get you to settle down, but he was wrong. That's why he left you." Ben sneered. "You and that damn career of yours. That's all you ever thought about. Why didn't you ever think about being a wife and mother? I would have given you that kind of life Savannah. I could have changed you. I could have given you everything. All you would have had to do was love me. Leave fighting the bad guys to the men. That's our job, not a woman's. Frank wouldn't have given you that life. Hell he couldn't. It was common knowledge that you were the brains in that partnership, Frank was just the brawn."

"That's not true!" I lashed back, jumping from the chair and heading into the great room. I had to put some distance between us. Ben leapt from his chair and followed me into the room, never taking his eyes off me.

"Frank and I were partners in every sense of the word" I threw out at him. "I loved him. He was everything to me. How dare you take that away from me! How dare you, how dare you!" I screamed as I lunged across the room at him.

Ben caught me in his arms and pushed me away striking me hard across the face with the back of his hand. I let out a painful yelp as I landed on the floor. I scrambled to my feet.

Things seemed to move in slow motion after that. Ben pointed his gun at me and took aim. I saw Jim come through the front door and Rambo coming at a dead run around the corner of the hallway and launch himself at Ben.

I pulled the other gun from the waistband of my jeans and heard myself scream "No" as I squeezed the trigger.

EPILOGUE

▼

I watched with great sadness as Cal wheeled Ben's body out the door on a stretcher. I had wanted to take him alive, make him pay for what he had done. In a way I guess he had.

Jim, the Chief and the entire task force were now assembled in the great room of my home. I sat numbly wrapped in a blanket on the couch. For some reason I couldn't stop shaking.

Sydney and Rambo had curled up at my feet and were happily munching on a treat that someone had given them.

Jim was sitting next to me stroking my hair and whispering in my ear that it was over and everything would be all right now.

But he was wrong, nothing would be all right again, ever. I had taken another life. Granted it was in self-defense, but that gave me little solace at the moment. In my eyes I was no better than Ben; just more controlled. Maybe in the end Ben had won.

The Chief handed me a glass of wine and knelt down in front of me on the couch.

"Listen Savannah," he said gently, "I have this little cabin up north. It isn't much, but you are more than welcome to take the dogs and get away for a while. Kind of regroup if you know what I mean."

"Thank you Chief." I responded, squeezing his hand. "I will think about it. Right now I would really appreciate it if everyone would leave. I really need some time by myself"

"If that's what you want Savannah," Jim said with a hint of disappointment in his voice.

After everybody left, I wrapped myself in a blanket, curled up on the couch and put on a tape of Casablanca. It had been Frank's favorite movie. I then proceeded to have a good cry. Something that was long overdue.

A week later I found myself packing the dogs and a suitcase in Jim's Durango and heading for the Chief's cabin up north.

Jim and I had talked frequently during the past week and had decided to give our relationship another try. But we had a lot of things to talk about first. I had my doubts, but lately I had doubted a lot of things.

Perhaps the Chief was right. Maybe I just did need time to regroup. Only time would tell.

0-595-25900-6

Printed in the United States
832500001B